Blood Crow

V. DOMINO

Blood Crow

V. DOMINO

Blood Crow

Copyright © 2020 by V. Domino

Cover Design: Books and Moods
Interior Formatting: Sinfully Seductive Designs

FIRST EDITION

ISBN: 979-8-5507414-2-9

10 9 8 7 6 5 4 3 2 1

To all dark hearts.

WORLD OF THE Crow

Blood Crow or Vocem Sanguinis: A race of vampires that were created with black magic.

True Crow: A title belonging to the Crow sisters only because they are the only direct descendants of the Original Vocem Sanguinis, William Crow.

Hellhounds: A race created when witches use black magic to kill a human. Their souls are bound to dogs.

Supernatural Elders: Clan leader of every race, minus the Blood Crows

Vincula: Hell's prison for those who are immortal.

Chapter ONE

L ife is said to be the best teacher. It teaches you right from wrong through the choices and decisions made by those who have gone before you. But history is easily forgotten, twisted and repeated.

If history were a person, she'd be a repetitive bitch.

Our youth is supposed to be the most enjoyable and memorable time in our lives; the teen spirit. Yet on the flip side of that coin, those same years throw lessons at you and in order to survive you'll need to learn them.

But I've been alive for almost two hundred years and I've yet to learn the lessons regarding the heart.

Now, I'm not talking about familial love. That I have in plenty when it comes to my sisters. No, I'm talking about a life partner, your other half, your right hand. Your ride or die…

But that type of love is so frail. In my opinion, at least.

It's capricious and slippery, easily swayed with a misconstrued look or dismissive gesture. At the snap of the fingers, a simple word can cut or bruise it. In the short span of a second your true love can go from loyal to disloyal. Weakened by the temptation of curvy figures or the sultry smile of another.

I've seen the roaming eyes of those *true loves*… hugging one while lusting over another. Fuck that pain.

That's why I've never considered learning such lessons. I don't need the love of a man; I don't need anyone's love but my sisters. So, as I sit here and watch these humans cry and mourn over heartbreak, self-induced I might add, I scoff at the notion. It's the same thing every time. The cycle history refuses to give up.

History would also be a vain hag, showing her old face any chance she gets.

Monotonous and oh so annoying.

"You're leaving me? Please, you can't go. I love you." My lips move in sync with the crying adulterous husband as I eye my black fingernails. Jeez, I really need to repaint them.

"You're nothing but a cheating liar, Steven!" I continue my lip sync as the heavily pregnant woman snatches her keys and walks out the front door, slamming it on the groveling asshole.

Honestly, I've seen the same story many times over, I can probably act it out too.

You see, Steven here is a womanizer. Normally, I have no qualms with someone doing their own thing, be it promiscuity or celibacy, I really don't care. To each their own, right? But when it comes to marriage and making vows before witnesses? That's where a line should be drawn and obliged.

Steven made a promise to love and cherish his wife, not every hole on the block. He should have the decency to keep the promise he made or man up and break off the marriage. Instead, he fouled her womb with an offspring who will most likely continue a shit cycle.

I may not have a romantic bone in my immortal body but in my humble opinion, only selfish people fool around with the heart. Sneaking around and piling up the lies will eventually bite you in the ass.

But what do I know, right? I've never fallen in love. Don't plan to either.

I wait in my cloaked shadows as Steven calms down from his insincere crying fit. My shadows are invisible to the human eye but if a mortal were to get too close to me while I'm cloaked, he would feel a cold spot. While my kind is cloaked we are untouchable by humans but we can touch them and all their worldly possessions.

It's quite the tool we have in our arsenal.

So here I am lounging in the living room that's for display only, with my Demonia Trinity boots propped up on his ugly modern glass coffee table. Too bad he doesn't see my dark red painted lips pulled into a wide smile as I watch his meaningless tears fall down his cheeks.

I'm not a ghost if that's what you're thinking. No, I'm a creature that has been inaccurately described by authors and movie makers since Vlad Dracula, who by the way was just a crazed man who knew how to kill a foe with finesse.

I'm a Vocem Sanguinis, a *Blood Crow*.

We're like the Vampires people once believed in, only much better. You see, the stories of blood drinkers date as far back as the seventeenth century but as time went on, the stories got twisted a bit. Like the bat stories. Yes, we can shapeshift, fully or partially, but we're not limited to bats only. As long as we've drunk it's blood at least once, we shift into any creature but our true familiars are crows, not bats.

I'm not too sure why that is, I think it's because of the curse the witches placed upon my human ancestors. It was made with the blood of crows. Whatever the case may be, we're bigger than your average crow, us females have a wingspan of six feet and the men have one of around eight feet in length.

So yeah, most of the folklores got us wrong but in each tale there's one fact that is true. For example, we can come out during the day but because of our sensitive eyes we prefer the moon to the sun. We can survive off of human food--but personally, I prefer a human *as* my food. We can be wounded and spells can be cast to hold us in captivity for eternity but the only thing that can kill us is hellfire. We can also walk amongst you humans but we choose not to because the supernatural world vibrates at a different frequency than the human world. This means that in the human world, every super looks clearer, sharper. It's like an SD movie compared to an HD movie; the difference is obvious and it causes unnecessary attention.

Steven draws my attention from the obnoxiously artsy furniture when he stands from his place at the table and walks over to the mini bar in the back of the dining room.

Ah, liquor.

Steven's best friend when he's feeling particularly sorry for himself. I watch as he drinks tumbler after tumbler of the amber liquid. I know his limits better than he does and he's passed the point of no return.

How do I know this? When I'm not pulling a hit with my sisters I like to people-watch. Being a bounty hunter for the

4

supernatural world is not as time consuming as one might think. We don't sleep so we have hours in spades and being immortal gives us years and years of time to fill. I got bored one night, so I decided to take a stroll through this neighborhood, looking for a fun snack when I saw Stevie over here, sweet talking a woman on the phone. I had decided I'd leave him alone since he was obviously loved and in love. I stood there watching his pulse race with the sweet sentiments coming from the woman on the phone when another woman came out the front door. Steven's loud heartbeat skipped and stuttered as he hung up the phone quickly.

Ahh, a triangle. What a cliche. I thought to myself.

Needless to say, I was pissed with my decision to let the lying scumbag live. After that I enjoyed the obstacles Steven had to face with his lies. Using my abilities, I started fucking with his life; unlocking his phone and leaving it in the room with his wife or dialing the mistress' number and putting it on speaker while Steven kissed his ignorant wife.

So yeah, I've been devious and manipulative lately-- playing with my food if you will--but he deserved it.

Steven continues drinking, ignoring the fact that he'll have a horrible hangover come sunrise. I guess it's no problem since he'll never wake up and beg his wife to forgive his unfaithful ass. He won't get the chance to spew his fake promises because tonight he will die. He'll be my dinner tonight and a daisy pusher tomorrow.

I stand from the cream colored couch and watch as Steven takes out his phone. Sending out sorry texts to his wife before texting his mistress. *Pig.* And my sister Rory has the audacity to ask me why I find love to be a joke. Here's you neon sign, babe.

Before he can get his sluggish fingers to unlock his phone I let my cloak dissipate and watch as he stumbles backward when my sudden appearance frightens him.

"Aw, what's the matter, Stevie boy? Thought you were all by your lonesome self, did you?"

I slowly walk over to him watching his eyes flare with desire as he looks me up and down from my long legs to my black and white hair. I'm not wearing anything too revealing, just fishnet pantyhose under my frayed cutoff shorts and my tight white tank top but the clarity of my form makes my otherworldly beauty more desirable.

The chains I have hanging from my belt clink together as I sway my hips with each step until I stop a foot away. I lean in close to his face and let my partially shifted snake tongue slip out from between my smiling lips and come close to his face without actually touching. I inhale the scent of fear and apprehension that floods his system, including that beautiful vein pulsating on his neck.

Emotions change the essence of a human's natural flavor. Hatred makes the blood taste like black coffee, bitter and harsh. Desire causes many different flavors, it depends on the type of desire the mortal is feeling but it can range anywhere from cocoa to a fruity flavor.

My favorite is fear. It's the sweetest emotion of them all. Honey and powdered sugar or cinnamon and brown sugar. But this, admittedly, handsome man before me has been drinking so his blood will taste delightful *and* give me a good buzz.

"Wh- who are you? What do you want?" I mimic his words while he speaks them; typical human. Why are these the only sentences a human mind can come up with in these situations? Why not say something more creative? Not that it'll stop me, but still, a little less predictability would be much more fun.

I step away. "Forgive me, handsome, I forgot my manners at the door. I'm Ronny Crow." I give a curtsy right before cloaking myself. He jumps again looking around the room in a panic. Once he stops and rubs his eyes, thinking he's just drunk and hallucinating, I reappear behind him.

"And I just stopped by for a little fun."

Steven jumps and spins at the feel of my voice kissing the shell of his ear. I don't normally play with my prey but this dirtbag deserves it. My sister Roxy is the one with a taste for *theatrics,* as Rory calls it. But once in a while, I like to have a good time too and watching this heartbreaker fumble around for his phone is my definition of a good time.

As he crouches to grab the phone he dropped, I kick him on his hip and hear the bone snap. Did I forget to mention that I'm stronger than even the strongest human? I am. My whole race is and most of the underworld is as well. The only race not stronger than the humans are demons. Well, technically they are but they're a cursed race who can't harm a human without invitation. They can't even enter a home unless there has been an invite from a family member within the last six generations.

Steven howls in pain as I squat next to him with a smile.

"The fear running through your veins is divine... it makes my mouth water."

I disappear again and reappear on his other side. Inches from his ashen face, I let my snake tongue slither out as I grab him by the neck and lift him up off the floor.

I feel my eyes change from they're normal blue to full on crow black. The pupil bleeds outwards covering my whites as I hiss.

"Let me have a little taste, mortal."

Before he can scream, I sink my teeth into his artery.

Sugared bourbon.

Cotton candy fear.

My favorite.

Chapter Two

O nce I'm finished with my cotton candy, or Steven as it were, I teleport home and dig out my ringing phone. I see it's Darren, my boss.

"Yeah?"

"French Quarter," he says before hanging up.

Darren is like a father to us Crow sisters. He's an old as hell sióg, *fairy*, but don't let the name of his race fool you. Fairies are vicious creatures with boundary issues. Darren has never told us how old he is but there are legends about him that date as far back as the Viking raids.

Fairies never physically age after thirty years old and each sub-race resembles an element. Darren is from the fire line so when he doesn't have his human glamor on, he's completely red with the tips of his pointed ears lit with fire and though he can cast any elemental spell, he's best with fire.

He also has one hell of a short temper so instead of dragging my feet, I grab my stiletto daggers and yell for my oldest sister.

"Yeah! I'm coming, shit." Rory's breathless voice comes from down the hall.

"That's what she said!" I yell back.

Ignoring my dirty joke, Rory comes through the doorway looking as frazzled as a preacher getting a lap dance.

"Did you get the call too?" I ask as I'm pulling on my thigh straps. I don't know what we're facing so I grab my vials of basic potions, the only kind I know how to make.

"Yes, I did. Roxy is already in the Quarter so grab the stridor." *whistle.*

As the leader of our group and family, Rory is always put together, but right now she looks like a mess. Her silver hair is in disarray and she keeps patting herself like she's looking for car keys.

"You want me to grab your scythes?" I ask with a cocked brow as I finish buckling my straps. What the fuck is up with my sister? This is not like her at all.

"I, ahem. Uh, yeah... I'll just get the damn things myself, Ronny. Geez. Always with the questions." I don't get to say anything because she stomps out of the room.

Ooookay.

She's acting way out of character. It reminds me of the time Roxy came out of Rory's bedroom with a video of Nymphs getting their freak on. I couldn't stop laughing when Roxy held up the Elf made 3D video cube playing the porno.

Rory is a terrible liar. She stumbles over her words and sputters like it's her job to let everyone around her know she's hiding something.

I wonder if she's seeing someone?

Recently she confessed she's lonely and wants a mate. She's not looking for someone to fuck, she wants someone who'll fit with her. Someone to come home to, someone to share her bed with.

I love my sisters with every fiber in my being. I'd take their places in hellfire without a second thought so when Rory told us this my heart clenched.

I want to make her happy. She's been everything for Roxy and me.

Rory became our mom and dad when our parents packed up and left us a year after Roxy was born. She made sure we were fed, clothed and protected. So if Rory wants a mate, I want to help her find him. She wants children? I'll buy her a hundred fertility spells.

Anything to see her happy.

The feel of magic weaving around the house breaks me from my thoughts while Rory's voice echoes in my head as she teleports herself to the Quarter. Yep, that's correct, we can mind-speak.

I got my scythes, we'll meet you there.

Oh yeah, Rory is definitely hiding something.

Alright, sister dear.

I throw in as much sarcasm as I can into the thought.

I grab the whistle at the last second, the silver sphere is covered in runes that really come in handy during a fight. Whispering the name of the supernatural race you're facing while tracing the rune with your finger causes the sphere to emit a piercing whistle only audible to that specific race. It'll knock out anyone within ten feet of it and give us plenty of time to overpower an enemy.

Once I have everything I need, I whisper the teleport spell.

"Corvos copulare." *Join the Crows.*

V. DOMINO

The Latin words take me wherever my sisters are, which happens to be the butterfly garden in the French Quarter of New Orleans.

Nola is home to most of America's supernaturals because the nightlife calls to us more than any other city in the country. Plus they have fantastic food. Human and otherwise.

I appear next to Darren who is glammed up, looking all GQ human. He still retains his height, build and basic bone structure but of course his skin and eye color are human-like.

"What's got you in a fire, Darren?" My pink haired sister asks with a childlike giggle. Being the youngest, Roxy doesn't have a single care in the world. She is the kind of girl who'll enjoy the rain while everyone else runs inside to stay dry. She's also a bit psychotic.

Bubbly and looney. Harley Quinn, if you will... minus the baseball bat.

Rory has always been a little worried for her because she thinks she somehow messed up while raising her. She didn't though. Roxy is perfect. So what if she giggles like a creepy child and skips around singing her own fucked up songs--like the one about guts and dolls. That doesn't mean there's something wrong with her.

Darren huffs at Roxy's fire joke, cause you know, fire fairy and all that. Clever.

"There's been reports in the human news that abnormally large dog-like beasts have been spotted roaming the Quarter. The human police have done checkups but nothing more, I'm sure they think it's pranks or drug induced callers. We've questioned clan leaders and the heads of races but no one knows anything."

"How about the Werewolves? Have you spoken to Freda?" Freda is a badass Werewolf queen. She keeps her race in check and her people only change on the week of the full moon.

"I've spoken to her but none of her people were in the city during the sightings plus they look like large wolves. These creatures have been described as *beasts*."

"Did you question the witches? Maybe they conjured something on the last moon."

Everyone looks at me like I've lost my mind. I roll my eyes.

Power, like the kind the witches have, can go to a person's head.

"What?!" I ask. "It's not like it's impossible. One wrongdoing and a witch can create an entire race out of vengeance." Darren nods but the pity filled look he has in his eyes makes my lip curl. I don't need pity, I love my life and abilities. I'm just saying… Witches are like any race, they can seek justice but the difference between witches and everyone else is that they have incredible powers.

We Crows know firsthand what they can do. Although, the original Crows deserved the justice the witches gave.

Many, many years ago a human, William Crow, and his followers were rounding up the witches in the village. He was murdering anyone who was accused of witchcraft or being anything other than a human and though he killed fifty-four people in total, none of them were actual witches. But then one night he finally caught an actual supernatural, only this one was just a baby.

Elsie was the two-year-old infant of the Hound family and she was spotted making a rock float in the village square while her family sold the deer meat their hunting dogs caught. In retaliation to Crow's despicable murder of the infant, a curse was placed on the Crow family and all those who followed William, making them the very things they hunted.

Immortals.

The entire Hound family died to create the curse, giving up their lives while turning the Crows into the immortals they hated. Effectively turning them from hunters to prey.

After years of being on the run from both humans and witches, the original Crows were caught and put into eternal captivity deep in the bowels of Hell's vincula. *Jail.*

Unlike the despicable William Crow, the supernatural world leaders let the children of the families live freely. After years of good behavior from these children, the leaders partially broke the curse, allowing any future Blood Crow offspring to have a wider food source and special abilities such as cloaking, teleportation, strength, speed and telepathy within bloodlines and between bonded mates.

Despite the fact that witches haven't been hunted or killed since the original Crows, I still have a feeling they're brewing something. Perhaps that's what this supernatural dog is.

"I've tried contacting their leaders but since gaining new leadership, the witches spend most of their time off the grid. Finding them is difficult." Flicking his wrist, a file appears in his hand. "I pulled the records of the 911 calls and used their description of the creatures to check our archive files. I believe I've figured out what these creatures are."

He hands over a manilla folder with the word *Hellhounds* across the top.

"This is the only file we have on the race but they've not been around since the first Crow."

I snatch the file from him and flip it open. The first thing I see are hand drawn pictures of what looks to be doberman pinschers but upon closer inspection of the sketches, I see holes along its body. Similar to fish gills. They're broad and muscular but they also stand much taller than the sketched dog next to it.

Hellhounds are host to many different stories but the truth is, they were the enemies of the original Crows. They're rumored to be the bringers of death, that's true but the only deaths they cause are of my kind because Hellhounds control Hellfire.

It's said that when the Hound witches died casting their spell on the Crows, their souls were bound to their hunting dogs. No one knows how true that is but it's believed because William Crow and his followers were hunted and stalked by the animals. Other stories say that because of the dark spell they casted, the souls of the witches were bound to the hounds of hell and never found Elsie again. Therefore, the Hellhounds began hunting and killing Blood Crows in order to quell their need for retribution.

Whatever the truth is, it doesn't matter much, if Hellhounds are here that means my sisters and I are in danger. We're the only True Bloods in New Orleans.

"This file is useless, Darren. It says nothing helpful. How do we find these creatures and kill them?" Rory asks while tightening her grip on the scythe at her side. Its vicious blade has tasted blood from almost every creature in the supernatural world.

Darren heaves a sigh and before answering. "You can't kill them. They're creatures from hell."

My first thought is, *oh fuck*. My second thought is, *fuck that.*

"But they can be immobilized with spells. I've got my team working on the ingredients as we speak."

Well, that's very fucking helpful.

There's no way I'm going to let these mangy pups hurt my sisters. I'll find a way to kill the fuckers. Every creature has a weakness. I'll find theirs and I'll exploit the hell out of it. I've lived too many years, seen too many things, and survived too many wars to be taken out by a mutt with a centuries old grudge that has zero to do with us.

Hell no.

Looking at my sisters I see the same determination. Rory's eyes have gone completely black with a silent snarl on her pretty face as she looks between us.

"Let's go hunting sisters."

Chapter THREE

Darren gives us a few more notes on his research but still, it's nothing too useful. It seems the most we can do is trap the mutts and hope the witches can cast them back to their guard posts in Hell.

I don't see that working though. If these are the Hellhounds of old, they wouldn't be topside unless....

"What if someone conjured them?" I ask after Darren pops out of existence. He's heading back to headquarters to continue his research. Plus, he knows we don't like for him to hover while we complete a mission. He becomes that annoying backseat driver you want to run over.

Roxy giggles while her ram horns grow out and curl behind her head as a huge manic smile splits her face.

"I hope so, I love challenges," she says as she swings her iron-spike ball and chain.

"You're right, this is going to be fun." I jump high off the ground and shift. My crow's eyes are sharper and have night vision. Perfect for hunting these pups.

My flight takes me around the quarter multiple times, seeing nothing between the buildings. I continue to fly, swooping low and landing on Rory's scythe as she slinks through the darkened streets.

After skipping along the streets humming her lunatic's tunes, Roxy is now walking along the rooftops while I rest my wings. I don't get tired easily, but I haven't fed as much as I'd have liked so keeping my energy is a priority, especially if we do find these dogs.

Using our telepathy gifts, or *sister speak* as Roxy calls it, I say into their minds,

Did you see anything in the file about their sleeping habits or where they like to sleep?

I didn't read the files but if I were a stinky, fleabag dog from hell, I'd sleep somewhere hot. Someplace that smells and feels like home. In their case, maybe a dumpster that's been lit on fire.

Roxy's silly words make sense, in a nonsense sort of way.

Roxy's right. Let's get inside the greenhouse. The place is humid and warm, even in the fall season. I'm about to shift but Rory stops me.

Wait, teleport in there in crow form. Stay high and report their location if they're in there.

I hop off her blade and fly around the building, trying to spot movement or, you know, a large mangy dog through the windows. I see nothing on this side of the greenhouse so I swoop around the corner.

As soon as I turn the corner I feel a shift in the air right before a big ass paw knocks me out of the air.

18

I shift before hitting the ground so that I can roll away fast. I jump to my feet and bring out my short swords. I let out a long warning hiss while searching the darkness for the beast that hit me. My eyes land on three sets of red eyes. No pupils, just red glowing eyes that watch me. They don't move so I take a moment to examine these three Hellhounds.

Found them, Southside of the building. Three big ass dogs.

They are huge! I stand at five feet, eight inches and I can easily see that I'm at eye level with the jaw of the largest beast. They're eerily silent too. I only know they're breathing heavily because of the plumes of smoke puffing out of their four-barrel noses. Their pointed ears twitch a millisecond before my sisters appear beside me. That tells me they'll have that second to know our moves, a slight second to predict and prepare.

"The Hellhounds have found us, sisters."

I don't take my eyes off the beasts as I speak so I catch when the second largest Hellhound flinches slightly, barely noticeable. The smoke from his nose stops as if he's holding his breath.

Then he moves, charging straight for me as the other two jump into action against my sisters. Even as Rory and Roxy move against the other two beasts while yelling obscenities. I stand there for a second—part shock and part admiration—as I watch this creature's muscled body flex with his movements. Shaking myself out of my stupor, I teleport myself to the spot he just vacated and whistle at him like he's a puppy.

"Here doggy, doggy. I'm over here boy." The beast spins in place and snarls at me. Can he understand me? I crouch quickly when the beast jumps high into the air, pretty agile for a giant dog, before shifting into a gloriously tattooed man and landing ten feet from me.

Oh. My. Fangs!

This unknown creature-man-thing is tall and muscular and *butt-ass-naked.*

Let me tell you, this guy was gifted with a body that can put the best male model to shame. He's mind-numbingly beautiful.

My eyes follow the tattoos that start at the sides of his head and flow down to his jaw. They're intricate and detailed but his face is completely blank, almost like he's nothing but a walking tattoo and his ink-free face is a mask. The ink flows unhindered down his sculpted body. I try not to stare at his dick but give me a break, man! You can't stand there naked and expect me not to stare.

I mentally wipe the drool from my mouth just as he softly snorts, making my eyes shoot back up to his face, straight to his olive green eyes that are blush inducing.

But that's not all, there's something tapping on my mind like an elusive memory knocking at the door.

Brows furrowed, I continue to stare into his eyes when suddenly it clicks. I don't know how it happens but somehow I see this guy's soul open up before me and it seems that he can feel it as well.

For just a couple of seconds, a kaleidoscope of different colors flash in my mind; emotions and memories all mixed into one body. I see tears that have fallen in misery and I see thunderous rage but I also see celebrations of victories and joyous moments with family. Each color is tied to the emotions of those memories. I blink and pull myself from this strange vision. *What the fuck was that?*

Swinging my eyes from him, I look around to my sisters, not that I have to check on them, they're deadly as fuck but I need to get my jumbled thoughts together. I was not expecting this.

Fuckity-fuck-fuck!

I see that my sisters seem to be fighting the same trance or maybe they're mentally drooling too. Holy hell, what do these hounds eat?

Like my man over here, these guys are gorgeously muscular and covered in detailed tattoos as well, only they don't *zing* for me like green eyes did.

The one staring at Roxy like she's his next meal, is downright wicked looking with a sinister smile plastered on his sharp face. Like a sexy Joker, without the ridiculous clown makeup. The other guy who is currently making Rory squirm in her tight pants is the coldest looking of the three men. His brown hair hangs over his eyes and he has his head tilted to the side like Rory is an abstract painting. He is absolutely mouthwatering.

Oh my crows, these guys are definitely dangerous and I definitely need a cold shower.

Movement from green eyes has me bringing my attention back to him. He stops advancing when I step back and into a defensive stance; right leg back with my hips slightly turned towards him. I bring my short swords in front of me, in a ready position. I don't know this man but I will not hesitate to cut his dick off if he comes closer.

And keep it, too.

The smoke that puffed from his Hellhound's nose no longer appears as this godlike man tracks my movements with keen eyes. I'm already stunned and off my game with the fact that this hellhound just turned into a beautiful naked man but then he speaks and I swear my lady parts sing with lust.

"Doggy? Now that wasn't very polite, *black bird.*"

My breath catches at the sound of his voice, the smooth accented timbre of it felt like a shock wave floating over my skin. He takes a few steps to me but stops four feet away. He sniffs the air like he's taking in my scent and for some crazy reason, my heart begins to race and desire rushes through me. It feels like I took an aphrodisiac. His eyes flare as he takes another inhale. I watch as the color drains from his face and his jaw slackens but then his voice rings out... in my head!

Mate.

I gasp and cloak myself. Nope. No fucking way. I didn't hear him, nuh uh.

Let's get the fuck outta here, sisters. I mentally shout.

Green eyes frantically searches the area and heads for Roxy who squeaks before cloaking herself. I don't move from my spot, I'm cloaked after all, but now all the guys are staring at Rory expectantly. Her guy snaps his teeth at his brothers in warning when they step too close to her. Like he's possessive of her.

"Where are they, *pigeon?*

Joker asks at the same time Green demands,

"Where's my black bird?"

Rory smiles at the men, "Catch us if you can, *pups.*" Then she flips them off with both hands before cloaking herself.

Once we're standing in the living room of our house, my sisters and I stare at each other in shock. No sounds except for our heavy breathing.

What the hell just happened?

My emotions and thoughts run rampant but my body stays frozen. Who was that? Why did I hear his mental voice? Can he hear me now? What did he mean by *mate*?

Round and round my thoughts tumble, like a hurricane destroying my thought process.

Interracial mates happen, that's not such a big deal but I don't *want* a mate especially not one who is my mortal enemy and is currently hunting me.

This is so fucked up.

"Did you hear his voice?" Rory asks no one in particular.

Since my thoughts are on myself and Green eyes, I assume she's talking to me so when Roxy says yes... I don't think, I don't consider what the fuck I'm doing, I just react to the intense jealousy and possessiveness that slams through me.

One moment I'm standing across the room, the next I have Roxy pinned to the wall with my blade to her throat.

"Mine!" I hiss in her face before realizing what the hell I'm doing. I drop my hold and jump back, letting my swords fall to the floor. "I'm so sorry, Rox. I don't know what that was. I'm sorry." I drop into a squat and rub my temples.

"It's all good, Ronny but just so you know, I was talking about the guy who's charming smile could melt the panties off a priest."

What the fuck?

There's so many things wrong with that sentence.

"I don't know about charming, more like demented," Rory mumbles.

"That's what I said, *charming*." Roxy looks completely looney for the guy.

I shake my head and stand up. "Can we focus for a minute? Green eyes said the word mate but he mentally spoke it. Not to mention, I just attacked my sister in a fit of possessive jealousy. What the hell is happening, Rory?"

Rory looks straight at me with the same confusion running through my own head.

"I don't know but let's call Darren. Maybe he's found more information."

God, I hope so. This handsome Cujo is messing with my head and I can't have that.

Chapter FOUR

"**W**hat just happened, Draven? Where did they go?" Drac asks as he moves around the alleyway, grasping the air in front of him like he'll grab ahold of the girl he was drooling over.

Not that I blame him, the little pink hair Crow was beautiful even with curled horns growing from her head. But the one who spoke to me, the one with black and white hair, like a woman with two sides. Yeah, she's the one who captured and held my attention.

More than that actually, her beauty is from a different era; feminine yet fierce. She had tattoos all over her body like I do, only not as many. Her skin was pale like she'd been kissed by the moon, and I can only imagine her blush while in the throes of passion. Her eyes had been fully black when she first shifted from crow to beauty but it was her voice that pulled on the embers of my soul.

Yes, even when her eyes changed to sky blue as she looked upon my human form, it was her voice that caused the fire within me to grow hotter and the heat they caused to rush through me is one I haven't felt in many centuries.

"They teleported, Drac."

Drac turns to look at Draven with a sardonic look on his face. "You don't say? I had no fucking clue!"

Rolling his eyes at Drac's sarcasm Draven says, "They're scent is lost to us in our human forms. Shift so we can track their magic." Draven's eyes glow red just before his hellhound comes forth.

Draven has been our alpha since we were new pups in the supernatural world but before we were hellhounds, we were a family of hunters with latent magic in our veins.

We lived in a different era. A time where the stars were our GPS and the sun was our clock. A time where hunting food and growing crops was how we survived and not a lifestyle choice or a passing fad.

We lived a good life, even through the plagues and diseases of old. We never spent time trying to fit a fashion or threw away our coins on the newest devices, not that I can really blame humans for that now. It's what they know. But for me and my brothers, simple is what we know and what we're used to. The world today is filled with so many distractions, it's a wonder the humans get anything done.

Although, I wouldn't mind taking a selfie with my black bird. Pulling my hellhound to the surface I think about what I'm not used to; this Crow. Why did my soul claim her? Is it set in stone or can I cut the binding? Do I even want to?

Stuck in a realm where space and time doesn't exist, I didn't have anyone but my brothers. Sure, there's other hellhounds in

Hell's Vincula, but there's no one there we have ever connected with on anything deeper than sex.

But my black bird... she saw me, all of me. Though I look like I'm still in my twenties, the same age range I was when I became a Hellhound, this Crow saw things deeper than my physical being. In the short amount of time we stood before one another, she looked into my pits of fire. She saw things no one has ever bothered seeing or was capable of seeing.

Feeling dead inside has been something I've grown used to but when her wide eyes touched my soul, I felt everything fall open like a book that had fallen from its place on the shelf. I felt when she sifted through all my pages, touching on each painful word of my past, reading each tear that's fallen in private.

Yet that's not the most shocking of it all. What truly had my embers burning brighter is when she liked what she saw, when she didn't snicker at my moments of weakness or show me pity. My hound laid claim without hesitation. I can't quite place the blame on my beast though, my black bird has me in her talons and I'd be lying if I said I didn't like it.

I growl at that. I feel weakened by this feathered beauty and these damnable feelings she's caused me.

I shake my head when Drac head butts me as he passes. I can't begin to explain what happened to me, did the same happen to them?

With Draven, who can tell, but Drac looks like he found a bone to hoard.

Pushing thoughts aside as best I can, I fall in step with my brothers, following the scent of old magic.

Jasmine and peppermint.

The smell would make anyone think of bath salts or aromatherapy but the witches of the past used them for brews. Non-lethal defensive potions contain these two herbs which makes me wonder why these powerful Crows are using brews that can be used by anyone without magic in their veins. The Crow sisters are rumored to be the most powerful Vocem Sanguinis, *Blood Crows*, because their kind was created with a witch's blood. Therefore, they're the only known immortal witches. That's the rumor anyway.

You see, our great grandmother was the only one in our family who cared for the craft. My brothers and I lost our *witchiness*, as Drac calls it, when we became the beasts of Hell. Though we still have superior abilities such as immortality and Hellfire.

My mother and father never wanted to learn how to use the magic lying latent in their bodies because at the time, witch hunts were rampant. Risking their family's lives for power wasn't worth it to them. They denied themselves but it was all for naught.

My brothers and I were out hunting when our grandmother, Merelda, found us and said that William Crow, the leader of the witch hunt, saw our baby sister using magic. All of his kills were done because of hearsay but with our sister, Elsie, he actually saw her using levitation. Her magic was just coming in but she wasn't in control of her own limb movements yet, much less her magic. The monster killed her along with other innocents. A baby, killed by a power seeking devil because she was giggling at a floating rock.

My mouth fills with venom at the thought of that vicious crime.

At the time, mankind would have seen William's deed as righteous. An act only allowed when the "criminal" is of the devil.

But let me tell you something, I've seen the soul within William and the rest of those vile witch hunters and they are the very essence of evil.

Enough, brother. Draven speaks into my mind.

I guess I let my thoughts slip past the mental barrier in my anger. One of the abilities we gained when we became Hellhounds. In our human life, we were a family who actually had magic but we chose to be law abiding citizens in our humble village and yet, William still took our most precious. In rage and despair, our mother and father chose to show William what true magic could do by casting our first and last spell as humans.

I'll never regret the curse put on those bastards even though our mother and father were lost to us. The spell took them and their souls; curses come with a price after all, and dark magic? That's the heaviest of them all. The spell came with everlasting consequences but losing Elsie was the most painful thing to ever happen to us, the decision to use the craft was an easy one. For many years after becoming Hellhounds, I often wondered how my mother and father were able to create a curse when they never practiced the craft, I guess a mother's scorn has no limit to her vengeance.

After our parents died, our grandmother saved my brothers and I by binding our souls to the bodies of our hunting dogs. I don't remember my human name but my Doberman's name was Drug so I took his name. Same with my brothers and their dogs.

During the transition from human to hellhound, we lost our witch abilities but we gained new magic. *Hellhound magic* and we became the hunters of the original Crows. We captured William and his followers but we let their children go free because they were innocent. It was the matriarchs of the Crows and the other

29

families, who needed to suffer in Hell. Using Hellfire, we sent their souls to Vincula and we were to be their eternal guards, but somehow my brothers and I were released from our eternal guard post.

We're not entirely sure how we got topside but we do know it took old magic to do so. Being that these Crow sisters are the most powerful immortals, they're our prime suspects.

Why would these Crows release us from our post and how? They obviously don't know how to use their magic... I don't smell anything on them but rookie potions and a very faint scent of craft in their veins. I tell my brothers as we cross through the city.

The scent is leading us to the outskirts of Nola. I want to ask him about connecting with my black bird and feeling my hound's claim over her but I'm not sure I want to acknowledge it to them yet. Plus, I can't reach her mentally so I'm not sure if we're truly bound to each other or not.

I smelled old magic on my—on the female who flipped us off. Draven sounds confused and his internal voice sounds like a snappy asshole. *Oh shit.* His words just registered.

Did it happen to you too?

Did your hound claim her?

Drac and I spout off our questions at the same time. Looks like we've all claimed a Crow for ourselves. What does this mean?

Answering my thoughts, Draven stops and spins around, facing us.

It means nothing brothers. They are still the descendants of our enemy, or did their pretty faces cause you to forget the suffering Elsie must have felt at the hands of William Crow? Stop thinking with your dicks so we can find these vampires.

Perhaps they've released us so that they can tie us to them and be used in some nefarious plan.

The plumes of smoke coming from Draven's nose and chest distort his face slightly but nothing can distort the anger in my words.

Fuck off Dray, you know damn well we'd never forget Elsie's pain. Fuck you for even suggesting that. Elsie was our baby sister, I'll never forget her.

Drac paces back and forth between us. He hates it when we fight but it's our way. All three of us are alphas, the only reason we let Draven lead us is because he is the oldest but don't let that fool you into thinking Drac and I are omega and beta. Hell no. We respect Draven and love him but no one is true alpha over me.

Brothers, now is not the time for dick measuring. Draven, your words are foolish and said without thought or care. Drug is right, forgetting Elsie is an impossibility. Two, William and his followers are the cause of her pain not these very fucking distant relatives. Pull your head out of your ass and don't lay the sins of one on another. We don't know how we were released so until we have actual proof I suggest you stop thinking with your fucking anger.

Draven and I stare at one another... in utter shock.

Drac never has a sensible thought nor does he have an ounce of sound reasoning. He's a chaotic being filled with manic cruelty. Cruelty that he finds soothing and joyous to his soul. He has never once offered placating words and he has never played the level-headed man he's being at this moment.

What? He asks with sincere confusion as he looks between Dray and I.

What has possessed you, a fucking monk? Draven's laughter rumbles through our heads.

Ah, no. Not a monk but a pink haired devil has made me see the light and I have an itch to see if her insides are just as colorful. Now stop fighting and lead me to my meal.

There's our lunatic brother.

Draven shakes his wide head before turning and following the trail once again. I understand Dray's hesitance but if our hounds claimed them, I want to find out why.

You're right, Drac. If there's one thing history has taught us, it's that one man's bigotry is not another's. I won't judge them based on William but I will try them and if I find them guilty— Dray stops as the trail ends at a large black plantation house. He turns around to face us as he shifts into his human form before speaking—"I will kill them."

Chapter FIVE

T he weeks have gone by quickly or slowly, depending on your perspective.

We've had no contact with the three Hellhounds nor have there been any police calls from the humans. It's as if they fell down the hole they crawled out of and I'm not completely sure how I feel about it.

On one hand, I'm relieved that I don't have to worry about the safety of my sisters. I don't have to worry that some hellfire wielding beast is after them. But on the other hand, I'm slightly, marginally, just a teeny tiny bit disappointed.

Okay, I'm completely disappointed. I think a good dog fight would have been amazing. I've never had the blood of a dog before but I wouldn't mind getting a taste of Green's fiery blood.

"You're going to blow yourself up if you keep mixing potions like that. Where's your head at, Roxy?"

Rory's voice pulls me out of my musings.

"You're one to talk, Ror. You broke the vials yesterday but you didn't see me complaining."

Rory opens her mouth for a comeback but I toss my blade between them, nailing the post behind them. Truth is, we've all been a little off our rockers since the Hound brothers disappeared and I for one am done being a simping bitch.

"Let's go out!" I clap my hands and try to put a little Roxy flavor into the suggestion. Rox always gets her way when she's all bubbly about something.

"No way, Ron. Those hellfire dogs could be anywhere just waiting for a chance to strike."

"Don't be a chicken shit, Rory. You've never run from a fight before, why now?"

I know I sound like a tantrum throwing brat but seriously? What is she so scared of? Three dogs are nothing for us. We once fought a rogue group of Blood Crows who were part of a rebellious faction. They believed they'd find salvation in starvation.

The five male Blood Crows were gone in the head, madness having taken over, and they began slaughtering humans without care. After my sister and I contained them, the elders took over.

That's the thing with the elders, they let us do their dirty work yet they still see all Blood Crows as the lowest kind of all supernaturals. Sentencing the Blood Crows to eternal damnation in Hell was a bit of an over kill if you ask me.

Seems that justice is always corrupt, no matter the race.

"She's not running from a fight, she's using it as an excuse to hide from that sexy man she's been panting over." Roxy tosses a vial stopper at Rory's head in her frustration and the little cork splatters goo across her brow.

Roxy and I howl in laughter, holding our stomachs at the homicidal gleam in Rory's eye.

"Fine, you two little rodents want to go out, let's go out but we're going to Club Libidine." Rory wipes her brow, gathering the gunk and rushes over to Roxy, rubbing her hand against Roxy's lips.

Whatever the substance was made of it makes Roxy's lips puff up bigger, making her natural bee stung lips look like Botox gone wrong.

I want to puke and laugh.

Laughing wins over especially when Roxy starts screaming and cursing in a rage. Even her screams are muffled behind those burger buns. The effects will wear off in a few minutes so she's freaking out over nothing.

I run out of the kitchen just as Roxy pulls out her daggers, looking to kill Rory.

Once I'm in my room I pick my outfit for the club.

Libidine is the hottest supernatural club in Nola. Latin for *lust,* Libidine is a sex club slash rave club. The owner, Mayfly, is a Nymph who has a wicked taste for Blood Crow, male or female. He has often tried to seduce my sisters and I but being bounty hunters for the Elders has allotted us certain potions that block hypnosis of any sort.

It's helpful against Mayfly and his seductions which is damn good too because if he likes how you taste, he'll tie you to him. Similarly to a mate binding but not quite.

Mates.

The word makes me think of Green eyes. I wonder where he went and if Rory is right and they're lying in wait for us to slip up.

I let out a growl and shove thoughts of Hellhounds to the back of my mind. Tonight I'm going to get fucked up, take some mushrooms and drink some spiked blood.

I grab my black slingshot bodysuit, blood red bondage leggings and black nightshade lace skirt then pair the outfit with my Scream Queen platform boots. The strappy outfit is very fucking revealing but at a blood rave, the less clothing, the better.

Two hours later, I'm snorting lines of Insania. A pink powder drug created with herbs and a special plant that only grows for witches. It's a mild hallucinogen and a major upper but ingest too much and you'll go insane, hence the Latin name. You'll begin to see hallucinations of your worst fears but these feel so real that you can't talk yourself down from the high.

"Oh! I want some, Ronny!" Roxy says as she appears next to me. I rub my nose and give her a skeptical look.

Last time I gave her some she ended up horribly injuring two Lycans by swinging her spiked ball and chain around doing her 'dance moves.'

Rolling her eyes she says, "It won't be like last time, I promise. I'll be a good girl." She throws in a big pout and whines like a puppy. Roxy always gets what she wants.

"Okay but I swear I will tell Darren what really happened to his Maserati if you get out of hand tonight."

Rory walks in and tosses us both our entry passes. They're bracelets that have been charmed to cloak the wearer. We don't exactly need one but it keeps up cloaked from humans while visible to Supes.

Snapping on the bracelets, we hold hands and teleport to Club Lust.

Walking into the club is sort of like walking through a veil. The building is hidden within the cloaking spell but once our bracelets touch the boundary line, the whole place is in view.

The entry is framed by the bright neon lips of a sexy Fae and walking through is like being swallowed into the otherworld of lust, ecstasy and euphoria.

Directly in front of us is the huge dance which is filled with the dancing bodies of almost every kind of species known to the Supernaturals, some of which are naked, all of which await the shower of blood soon to come.

The libidinous dancers dance erotically to the dubstep playing while my sisters and I make our way to the bar in the far right corner.

In the human clubs, hitting the dance floor to work up a thirst is often what happens but here in my world… you need to build up your sexual appetite with some drinks spiked with an aphrodisiac.

"Three Depraves and three Impures!" I shout to the bartender as Roxy bounces on the balls of her feet while Rory starts to move with the beat.

This is what we needed sisters. I tell them.

Yes! Now, let's get fucked up and find us some sexy men to taste. Roxy says enthusiastically.

I have to ignore the slight distaste I have for anyone who doesn't have tattoos and green eyes and judging by the way both of my sisters falter a split second… I think they feel the same way too.

"Fuck that. Let's have a well-deserved time and find some good dick!" Rory shouts as she hands us our shot glasses.

Completely unlike her but I won't complain tonight.

"Bottoms up Crows!" We shout in unison before shooting back the fiery liquor.

Quickly chasing the Impure shot with the Depraved drink, the fire in my throat soothes and soon the room begins to pulsate with the music. I toss the straw, chug the rest down, and grab Rory and Roxy's hands. They must've had the same idea because we all reach for each other.

Giggling like loonies, we make our way to the dance floor and shove others out of the way to get to the middle. Most people know us here and know our wicked reputation as the underworld bounty hunters so most move willingly.

Now, my sisters and I are close but we don't fuck around with each other sexually but when it comes to dancing? Let's just say we know how to seduce the men around us.

The music slows to a sensual beat, perfect for the carnal desire running through the veins of everyone around us. 'HDMI' by BONES begins to speed up with the rapid lyrics and as the beat drops everyone begins to jump and swing their glow sticks.

Fuck yes!

I shift into my crow and fly up to the industrial beams ten feet above our heads and shift back. Hanging by the back of my knees I let my glow sticks drop before spinning them to the beat of the music.

The dancers cheer louder when the club's dancers take my show as their cue to begin their pole dances. After a few more minutes, I drop from my position as a Fire Fairy begins to spin fire on stage. *I love this place.*

Everyone can let go of their masks and be who they want to be for the night. No judgement and no fouls. You are who you want to be and anyone with a problem can suck an egg.

I signal to my sisters that I'm headed to the bar but Roxy is jumping up the stage to dance on the poles while Rory continues her dancing with a Succubus named Gianna.

Getting to the bar, I order a glass of blood and mix in some of my Insania for a little pick-me-up. All that dancing has me feeling in need of it.

Just as I bring the glass to my lips, my eyes land on Mayfly as he scoots between my stool and the now vacant one next to me.

Mayfly is somewhat of a crime boss in our world. Living against the rules and laws of the Elders and running illegal businesses like he's untouchable, Mayfly has an air of unfiltered dominance. My sisters and I turn a blind eye to his deeds against the elders so long as he gives us useful information on other criminals. Usually they're his rivals anyway.

"Will you dance me for me, *Crow*?" He slithers out the name like a hissed sigh.

He's devastatingly gorgeous with his light cocoa skin tone and gray eyes. But he's like a demon; once he has you, you're nothing but a wonton addict, salivating for more of him.

"Hello, *degenerate*." I smile sweetly, flashing my fangs, "No, I will not dance for you."

He reaches over and waves his fingers in my face like he's a street magician who is about to pull a quarter from my ear but I know he's trying—and failing—to use his magic against me. I wink at him when the magical waves of his fingers stop moving and he sees it's no use on me.

But he's not deterred. He drops his hand to my thigh and moves on to the pleading part of his attempts. I can't say I'm not tempted. His luscious lips and sharp teeth are just begging for some action but it won't come from me.

"Don't you want to loosen up? I can show you things you've never seen before." Again with the hiss only now he drags his fingers up my thigh before hooking a finger in one of my bondage straps, "I can make you *feel* things you've never felt."

I'm about to break his wrist when a loud snarl sounds from somewhere followed by gasps and screams. I know that snarl.

The Hounds are here, sisters.

I see them at the entrance. They're headed towards you but Joker spotted me! Roxy says with glee.

Be ready! Rory shouts.

The crowd parts and three Hellhounds stand before us. Tongues of fire lick out from their open cuts as they bare their teeth.

I reach for my blades but before I can attack, the men shift.

In their place; three men, clothed like sexy bikers. They continue to bare their teeth at the people around us, threatening anyone standing too closely.

Green eyes is focused on Mayfly and how his hand grips my bicep in a possessive manner but all he does is push me behind him like I'm some fragile little bone the dogs want.

"Speak to my *mate* again and I'll rip your throat out, continue to touch her and I'll rip your worthless soul from your body." Green eyes looks like he's barely holding himself back but his words piss me off.

"I'm *not* your mate, *mutt*." I'm seething.

The people around us start to slowly go back to dancing and partying, the drugs flowing through their systems sway their fears back to euphoric levels but they keep an eye out on the men.

"You heard her, she's not your mate. Now I suggest you take your friends and get out of my club or I'll have you removed, piece by mangey piece."

Fucking men. Claiming women like property and then fucking off without care. Like the breeze in an open field; coming and going as they please.

I shove Mayfly out of my way as Green eyes completely ignores him and gives me a devilish smirk, "Not your mate, eh? Let's see."

Green grabs the arm of the closest girl and slams his lips to hers.

Just like what happened with Roxy, I attack with only one thought on repeat.

Mine!

Chapter Six

For weeks we watched the Crow house. For a full month or so, the Crow sisters stayed silent and on their property, within the boundary spell. We couldn't risk breaking through without alerting them but the separation was torture. Even with our strong hearing, we hardly ever heard them speak audibly.

Their silence was just as agonizing to us as not being able to see them.

Whatever happened when we first laid eyes on the three women has only grown stronger. Mate bonds are no joke but hearing rumors of it and enduring it are two vastly different things.

When it wasn't my turn to hunt for food, I watched through the windows almost every second of the day and night. Desperate to catch a glimpse of my Black Bird.

Yes, that's right, *my* Black Bird. There's no denying what has happened no matter how difficult it is to understand. Hell, even Drug has had enough of the distance between him and his silver haired Crow.

We made plans to attack the boundary spell tonight using our hellfire but then we heard the girls arguing and finally agreeing to go out to Club Libidine.

Quickly we changed our plans and made our way to this club after hitting a shop for these very constricting clothes. On the way here I had gone through many different scenarios on how to approach my Black Bird but hearing the Nymph try to seduce her... *I'm going to kill him.*

"I'm *not* your mate, *mutt.*" Black Bird's voice is so cold you can practically feel the air drop but all it does is make me smirk.

She really believes she's not mine. I think it's about time she faces her reality. Black Bird is mine until we break the binding.

My lips will be the only ones touching her skin. Her body will know only my rough hands. It will be my words alone that find her ears as I take her and only my body will bring her to euphoric heights.

Why? Because she's fucking mine.

"Not your mate, eh? Let's see." Without much care, I grab the nearest woman, a succubus, and slam my lips to hers.

I don't get the chance to ponder why this girl's lips, soft and pillowy as they are, make me cringe internally because Black Bird is ripping the girl's arms from my neck.

Hissing like a cobra, Black Bird holds the demon by the neck before lifting her off the ground completely. I must say, my little Crow looks delicious when her eyes are shifted black.

"Mine!" Black Bird snarls at the gasping demon before tossing her like a bag of bricks.

"Stop, Ronny! He's only goading you." One of the sisters snaps from behind me. I'm sure my brothers are keeping the Crow's claws back.

"Ronny…" I taste the name and looking at the wildly sexy woman before me, it fits her. "Looks like I *am* your mate." I smile as she curls her lips at me before charging at me for a fight.

Her speed is remarkable! If I were a human I wouldn't have been able to block her attack but I'm not human. With her fangs out, Ronny charges but I quickly wrap my fingers around her neck and squeeze.

Her skin is cool to the touch and as smooth as I imagined. Soft and pliable but not penetrable without magic. Her eyes stay blacked out but her pulse beneath my fingers is fast and erratic. I smell the anger on her but it's quickly becoming overpowered by desire.

Cloy and addictive. Her scent is fucking with my mind.

Along with her pulse, a vibration begins, like a cat purring with pleasure and I can't help the thought of shoving my cock down her throat while she does that.

Suddenly, said cock is in excruciating pain and the fuzz in my brain evaporates like the morning dew with the sun.

"I will rip your manhood from your body if you don't let me go, *dog*."

This fucking girl. I want to kill her and fuck her… Not in that order of course.

"Do it and I'll rip you and your sister's wings off before the night is done."

I don't wait for her to reply or follow through on her threat. Instead I push her back, pulling her fucking talons away from my balls, before slamming her back to my chest.

V. DOMINO

The music continued to play even through our interruption so I wrap my left arm around her waist and begin to move.

The music fades to a remix of Portishead's 'Humming,' which is one of their greatest underrated songs and the sensual melody is perfect for the vixen in my arms.

"Dance with me, Black Bird," I say into her ear.

I pull her harder into me and sway my hips side to side, letting her feel how hard I am for her... despite her attempts at castrating me. Her body moves smoothly, lazily, like a cobra swaying to the flute's hypnotizing notes. The song speaks of sex like poetry and Ronny is the embodiment of dark and sultry.

She doesn't push me away or fight me off; instead, she lets out a tortured moan and lifts her arms up her body slowly before gripping my hair and pulling my face down to her neck.

The erotic voice of the singer is arousing and anacreontic. It feels as if it's a tune laced with magic and the haze of lust fills my mind as it did moments ago. Improper and filthy thoughts buzz through my head, blocking everything else out.

I don't hesitate to act on what I want and what Ronny is giving, I bite her neck using my hellhound teeth. I sink them deeply and grind myself to her lush ass as she moans and gyrates against me. Her blood fills my mouth and though I'm not a natural blood drinker as she is, I still swallow deeply.

Magic laces her blood making the metallic tang taste like aged wine and fermented brew. Addictive and intoxicating. Her arousal shows not just in her movements or moans but in her aura. Her skin begins to glow and her hair floats upward as if caught in a breeze.

Her magic just came in... What the fuck did I just do?

I rip my mouth from her and watch as small sparks dance along her skin like tiny stars caressing her body. She turns around and faces me but just as they did in the alley a week ago, her eyes penetrating my soul only now they're white like an *Oracle's*.

"'I tasked you, Drug. Kill the Crows and be reborn.'"

Her voice is monotone and disembodied; not her own. She sways slightly like she's in a trance but then the music changes and suddenly there is a shower of blood pouring from above us.

Everyone cheers and begins to lick at the downpour and each other but my eyes stay on Ronny. Her face, now dripping in blood, looks far away but as I cup her cheeks she blinks the haze away.

"What was that?" She sounds normal but freaked out.

Before I can answer though, her eyes roll back and she begins to fall. Quickly, I scoop her up and call for my brothers,

Something is wrong with Ronny. I'm getting her out of here. We're right behind you, Drug.

In my arms, Ronny begins to convulse and mumble but I can't understand her with the music and moans of the bloody orgy going on around us.

Making it to the front doors, I kick them open and rush over to the river's bank under the moonlight and lay her down on the cool sand. Quickly I rip off my shirt and soak it in the water to clean her of the blood. The bite marks I left on her haven't healed and though she isn't bleeding, there are two punctures on her skin.

Did I cause this? Did I somehow kill the Crow with my bite? Fuck! It didn't feel like death though. It felt as if we were on a different plane, a new realm of magic and purity, but a bite from a Hellhound is deadly. Why the fuck did I bite her?

"What in the hell is happening to them?" Drac's frantic voice pulls me from my thoughts and it's then that I notice the other two Crows lying on the ground.

"Their magic came in. Somehow, brothers, we opened them up to their power source." Draven who is usually stoic and cold, wipes tenderly at his mate's neck where two puncture wounds are clearly seen.

"What happened when you bit her, Dray?"

Draven drops his head and tries to control whatever emotions are flowing through him but when he picks his head back up his eyes are the molten lava of his Hellhound.

"She said what grandmother always said to me, 'Draven Hound, you are a stain upon your name. Forever you will be a taint, a humiliating shame.' Then she fainted."

As the words are spoken, grandmother's face flashes in my mind's eye. I haven't thought of that old cow since I was a child but every word is correct. How would this Crow know about that? What powers do these creatures possess?

"Drac? What did she do or say?"

Drac shakes his head then tosses the shirt he was using on the pink haired Crow. The wounds on her neck stand out as well.

"I was lost in a haze, hypnotically so. I moved without thought and drank from her neck but then zaps of energy ran along our skin so I let go. She turned to me and said, 'Drac and his brothers have yet to complete the task we've given, the Crows still walk amongst the living."

This is fucking confusing. What does this mean? Then it clicks.

"Past, present and future." Is all I say as I point at each of them, "But how did we start this? Our bites are deadly and will kill anyone, even a demon. Not only did we fuck up by allowing ourselves to bite them but now we apparently have enemies."

"At least we know though," Drac says scooping up his mate, "Let's get them back to their house. We should be able to pass through their wards with them."

Fifteen minutes later we pass through their boundary lines and into their home. The plantation style home is enormous and filled with Victorian style furniture and decor. I wonder if it's from their century?

We lay the girls down on the more modern sofas and look around ourselves, unsure of what to do. We don't have long to wait though because all three girls come to like a switch was flipped.

"Rise and shine, birdies. Looks like your powers came in and you three need to explain your visions."

Perhaps I could have been a bit more gentle with these flighty birds but it seems that my brothers and I are on a time limit from an unknown enemy and I'd like to know who they are.

"The elders want us dead." The pink haired Crow says, looking straight at Drac with rage and sorrow in her eyes, "And you three are tasked for the killing."

It's quiet for a moment until Drac speaks up, "I think I want to see how slowly an Elder burns."

My eyes are on Ronny though. Does she think I will try to kill her? Do I want her to think I will? Fuck!

She leans in closely, her eyes glittered in black and her whisper sounds like a hiss, "Let's play a game called toss the bones."

Chapter SEVEN
DRUG HOUND

Toss the bones is apparently a reading on one's life. The way the bones fall and their placement can tell the reader what's to come in the person's life, sort of like tea leaf reading. I'm always open to knowing what's around a darkened corner in my life but we're waiting on someone else to arrive.

So here I sit, watching Ronny move around the kitchen gathering ingredients for her herbal tea and it will go down as the craziest moment in my life. She barely has anything on, not that I'm complaining but the sexy gothic look she has going on is at odds with the kitchen. It feels as if a grandmother should be in here baking cookies, not this Elvira meets Dominatrix.

The room is white with dark grey trimming and soft white lace curtains flowing with the breeze from the open windows. Ronny has dry blood all over and her black and white hair is knotted and tossed into a messy bun.

I guess I can't say much though since I'm sitting here shirtless with blood caked on my skin.

She catches me watching her as I sip from a mug with a fucking black kitty tail for a handle. How my life went from the fiercest creatures in hell, feared and rumored about to a man sipping from a pussy mug that says 'Bite Me-ooow' is completely beyond me.

"Why are you and your brothers here?" She sounds completely sincere and if I hadn't already seen her gift of seeing the future, I'd say she had nothing to do with us being released from hell.

"If I answer you, you have to answer my question." I'd answer anyway but I want to know why the hell my hound chose her as a mate.

"Deal."

I watch her lift a very nondescript mug to her smirking plump lips as I answer. *Fucker.*

"We're not sure why we were released or who did it. Well, we weren't until tonight. One day we're in hell guarding post as usual and the next instant we're back in Nola without permission to leave. We were sent there to guard our enemies and your ancestors so we figured the best place to find answers was the famous Crow Sisters."

Ronny continues to sip, thinking over my answer and her body is relaxed, no deceit or worry tainting her jasmine scent.

"My turn. Why do you use such rudimentary potions instead of your magic?"

I've been curious about the answer since the alley. Why spend time making elementary mixtures that won't do much when she can weave intricate spells to do so much more?

52

"Rory, Roxy and I are not witches, Drug. We're Vocem Sanguinis. We don't have those abilities." She says it like I'm an idiot in need of a head check.

My brows hit my hairline at that. I've heard the rumors of these sisters and the line of the original Vocem. Everyone in the underworld tells the tales of their ancestors with fear and wonderment. Someone has either been lying to these girls or the rumor mill is nothing but stories to pass time.

"What?" She asks in annoyance.

"Where is the love of your parents? Did they not teach you about your abilities?"

Ronny scoffs, "Love is for suckers, Drug."

My brow furrows and she opens her mouth once more but before she can say anything else, there's a crackling in the air like magic is being used. Immediately, I'm on my feet ready for an attack.

"Calm down, *dog*. It's just Darren." I curl my lip and growl at the little magicless girl. Soon I'm going to have to teach her how to keep her pretty little mouth closed or put it to use around my cock.

Turning my back to her, I head into the living room where I hear my brother addressing someone.

"This is Darren Ignis. He is our boss so he can help us find answers." Ronny says as she walks over and hugs the man. I don't like him.

He's tall with red skin and fire on the tips of his pointed ears. His eyes are bright gold and are in total contrast with his inky black hair. He looks like what humans depict has the devil only he's in a suit and doesn't have a pitch fork.

"I am Draven and these are my brothers, Drac and Drug."

Darren nods but looks to the Crows, "You three okay?"

I bristle at the question and I feel my brothers tense beside me, "Why the fuck wouldn't they be okay?" I ask through gritted teeth. Who the hell is this guy?

"First off boy, I can ask my girls whatever the hell I want when I want, got it? Secondly, you three are supposed to be extinct, not roaming around Nola striking fear in humans and..." He abruptly stops speaking and sniffs the air before a shocked look morphs his features.

"You claimed my daughters?" His voice changes and sounds as if multiple voices are coming from him.

Wait, daughters?

"Whoa, whoa, Dar. Calm down. They're just as shocked about it too. This is why we called you," Rory says soothingly. This Crow has a mothering feel about her and it's obvious she wears her heart on her sleeve.

"Yeah, let's throw some gas on your flames, Dare Bear. Don't start a fire in my house again." The little pink haired, Roxy says with a crazy giggle. Damn, she's like the female version of Drac.

Darren calms down slightly as he looks at the girls fondly even while his fists stay clenched at his sides.

"I think you mean *water* not *gas*," Ronny says next to me while rolling her eyes.

"That's what I said, *gas*."

Everyone stares at her for a moment until Drac tosses his arm around her shoulders, "Definitely gas."

Ronny turns and sits on the couch, completely over the conversation, and pulls out an aged wooden box. Inside are various bones and crystals. Beneath them is a divination board with runes.

We all sit around her as she sets everything up and I take this moment to ask Darren my own questions.

"You call Ronny your daughter but where are their real parents and why haven't they been taught how to use their magic?"

Everyone stops moving to look between me and Darren. The man pinches the bridge of his nose before answering on a heavy sigh.

"Their parents left them when Roxy was just a baby and I met them when they were all just teens. No one has seen or heard from them since leaving. Same with *their* parents and every parent before them. At first I suspected foul play but the Elders decided that without proof of anything that no investigation was necessary and ruling that it must be the way of the Vocem Sanguinis; to leave their offspring when they are able to care for themselves. As for their magic, there are no familial books passed on from parent to child as is with the witches and their books of spells."

What do you think of this man, brothers? I don't fully trust him. He doesn't have the foul scent of lies but that doesn't mean he isn't covering his scent with magic.

I believe him but I think it would be wise to be cautious, Draven says.

"So you mean we have actual magic and no one thought it was acceptable to tell us? We could have tried learning on our own." Ronny's voice is filled with outrage and I don't blame her. Books or not, they have a right to know about their abilities.

"And how could you not try to teach us when we're putting our lives on the line while bounty hunting for the Elders? What if we could have done a lot more for others instead of handing out damnation like fucking candy?"

Darren sighs like this is a conversation he's been dreading. He looks pained to have upset the sisters.

"The elders forbid it because you don't know your power source. Every race has a power source. The Fairies and Fae have nature and elements. Nymphs have their own source within the desires of others while Witches have the spirits and the Wolves have the moon. You three have no known source."

My brothers and I look at each other, "Until now." Drac says with a smirk.

"What do you mean?" Darren asks with his brows furrowed.

Without thinking of what I'm doing or why I'm doing it, I grab Ronny's hand and lift it with her palm up and mine cradling from beneath. I couldn't explain to anyone how I knew to do this but I push my hellfire through and the ball of black flames passes to her hand from mine, hovering an inch off her skin.

"We are their source *and* their mates."

EIGHT

Hellfire. Is. On. My. Hand. And I'm completely freaking the fuck out!

"Woah! Does it hurt?" Roxy reaches out her fingers to touch the black flames but Drac rips her arms back while Darren screams for her to stop.

"How is this not killing me? Oh fuck, am I going to slowly die? What did you do, Drug?" I'm panicking yet frozen to my spot. I want to shake my hand like I'm a human with a spider crawling on me but I'm afraid to accidently throw the flame and kill someone.

Drug pulls his hand from mine and with his natural heat away from the bottom of my hand I'm able to feel the heat of the flame. It doesn't hurt me in any way but that still doesn't calm my fears. My blood is rushing and my breathing is choppy. Why didn't the flame die when he moved his hand?

"Calm yourself, Ronny. We control Hellfire with our minds. A panicked mind is chaotic therefore your fire will reflect that."

Okay, that is not helping at all.

V. DOMINO

Breathe, sister. You got this. Breathe and slow your thoughts. Rory's soothing voice fills my head.

"Yeah, Ron. Breathe in and out slowly and once it's gone we'll kick this poodle's hairy ass for acting without thinking." Roxy chimes aloud, making Drug snarl next to me. Her hiss in return makes me smile despite the fear.

I close my eyes and do as my sisters and Drug said, calming my mind and picturing the flame dissipating. As soon as I focus on the thought, I feel the flame leave my palm.

"Bravo, Ronny. You did good." Drug's praise makes me blush but to cover it up I punch him on the arm.

"Don't do that again! I could have killed someone!"

He shrugs like it's no big deal and his stupidly sexy smirk makes my heart flutter.

Through the blood and grime on him, I can see the yellow flecks in his green eyes and his long lashes make them pop against his tan skin. The scruff along his jaw is sexy and tempting, begging for my fingers. I remember feeling the roughness on my neck as we danced together. I've never, in my hundred plus years, been so turned on while dancing with someone.

His grip on my throat was tight enough to keep the oxygen to my brain from flowing and combining that with his very large and hard cock grinding against my ass... everything was so much more intense.

I squeeze my thighs together just thinking about it.

Judging by how his nose flares and his eyes glow, I'm guessing he knows where my thoughts went. The haze of lust becomes a bubble around Drug and I; a veil between us and the world and everything around us becomes insignificant.

A whispered, *oh shit*, makes me jump in my seat. I completely forgot everyone else, just the way it happened at the club. Looking at Darren I see he's staring at us in what can only be described as awe.

I look down at myself to make sure I didn't slip a nip in my hazy lust and that's when I notice the tiny sparks along my skin. It looks like little lightning bolts gliding along the peach fuzz of my exposed skin but it's gone quickly.

"You really are her source or maybe it's the bond that is her source. How can this be?" Darren draws a rune in the air while whispering a spell and quickly his glamor is in place. No longer red but smooth chocolate skin and light brown eyes. I'll never get over how handsome my adopted dad is.

Plopping down on the chair across from us, he says, "Tell me everything. From the moment the bond was started to now."

We spend the next hour and half going over every detail we can remember and the men fill in the blanks where we totally backed out. To say that I'm freaked about these new abilities is a gross understatement.

Having the gift of sight is most definitely not a known ability for Vocem Sanguinis. We have strength, cloaking and teleportation. Aside from that, we're not supposed to have magic... Unless that's what the Elders want us to think.

"What if the Elders are the reason mom and dad are gone? What if they've been imprisoned or worse?" Roxy asks.

"If you had asked me this a month ago, I wouldn't have entertained the thought but you three are oracles and your sight can be trusted. It's straight and not hidden in parables or riddles. Gifted oracles haven't been seen since the curse was partly broken by the

Elders some one hundred years after you boys captured William Crow and his followers."

Wow, so these guys really are the Hound Witches from the stories. How fucking wild is that?

"Why did you say my brothers and I were thought to be extinct?"

"Perhaps it's another fabrication from the Elders but you three, the Hound brothers, were said to have been dead alongside the original Crows. The tale is that the Hound brothers died once their vengeance was had. Yes, we know Hellhounds are well and alive but you three... are said to be dead."

Everyone stays quiet a moment, processing everything that's been said. It's not very surprising that this has happened but it's still fucked up that the Elders would lie about this. I mean, aren't they supposed to hold true to the beauty of each race?

"Why would they do this to us?" Roxy's voice is soft and sad; it fuels my anger. They took my little sister's sinister smile and replaced it with a broken despondent look. Out of us sisters, Roxy always loved doing the bidding of the Elders. She felt that one day, there'd be recognition for us and maybe then our parents would want her.

Rory and I never had the heart to burst her bubble.

"Because, Roxy. That's the way it goes with any higher power. Even in humans, those with power are always corrupt and cruel. They look down on half breeds and treat them like their blood is watered down."

I stand up and move around, pacing as I do when I'm agitated but my anger only grows.

"That's not the worst of it though. They see us as nothing at all. Vocem Sanguinis are a created race... made from black magic. Unblessed and impure; vile and an abomination! Our kind have to live on the outskirts of the supernatural world begging for scraps from the naturals. Bigotry and ignorance. That's why they do this to us!"

My sight is fading and I feel like I'm about to blackout. What the fuck is happening. Why do I feel like this?

"Black Bird!" Drug's voice is far away and I can feel myself trying to grasp at him but my arms won't move from my side.

Blinking the haze away I see I'm no longer standing in my living room instead I'm standing in a large circular room. The walls are made of some type of stone that looks like pearl or opal, the only light source is the opening above my head. I can't see what is through the opening because a blinding light is shining through.

The groan of an iron gate opening sounds and a woman in a long black robe comes in. She has the cowl over her head so I can't see her face but her voice is like sandpaper against my ears.

"I tasked you, Drug. Kill the Crows and be reborn."

What the hell is this? I know I'm having a vision again but who is this beast of a woman?

The robed woman moves her hands in front of her and whispers a spell making a ball of light float in her palm. There's a large ring on her thumb but I can't see it well and my attention is brought to the man before her.

Hanging against the wall is Drug only he's covered in fresh blood and open wounds like he's been flogged. Why isn't he healing or shifted into his Hellhound?

He lifts his face up and smiles at the woman in the most evil way possible and when he speaks, his voice is laced with the hatred of a thousand demons.

"I worry not, the Crows are coming with the Hounds in the rear. Your threats are for naught, your end is near."

Drug drags his eyes from the woman and stares at me right in the eyes. Can he see me?

"Drug! Drug, I'm here! Can you see me?" I'm screaming but I can't feel my mouth moving. My heart is pounding so hard I can feel my ribs shaking but the room begins to spin and fade. I try to keep my eyes on Drug but I can't see anything until my living room is now in focus.

"Oh fuck!" I groan and stumble forward into two arms.

I look up into Drug's glowing eyes and notice everyone is around us but the solace I find in his presence is profound.

"Oh my fangs, Drug. They're going to capture you and beat you! They had you chained to a wall that was made of some type of stone. It kept you from shifting and healing. You were bleeding and broken!" I drop my head to his chest overcome with a mixture of sorrow and relief.

"A woman in a long black robe was hurting you because you refused to kill us." I lift up my head and try to move away but he holds me tighter to him.

"And I won't. You're right, Black Bird. Love is for suckers but what we have... it's damnation." His eyes continue to glow but his words calm my fitful heart and his thumb, which draws soothing circles on my back, settling my raging mind.

"Were you able to see the woman's face or hear her voice?"

Drug lets me move but he doesn't let me go. He lightly grips the back of my neck and keeps his body close to mine, letting his warmth wrap around my cold bones.

"Her face was hidden but her voice sounds like an old croon in need of a cough drop." I try to think of every detail possible there wasn't much else though. "Oh! She had a big ring on her left thumb. It was the only jewelry I saw on her fingers. It was silver and looked like it could have been an insignia or crest of some sort."

Darren gets up and shows us his bracelet, the family crest for his race.

"Every race with a leader at the Elder's table has an insignia. Fairies have gold bracelets, Wolves have platinum necklaces Nymphs have silver bicep bands and witches have titanium rings."

"Of course a witch is behind this," Roxy says with an eye roll.

"Not just any witch, the *True Witch* elder... Merelda Hound."

Chapter NINE

DRUG HOUND

Family is a strange thing. You think that because you share blood and have lived a life together you know them inside and out. You can recall their smiles no matter how long time has passed or how long it's been since you've seen it. You can remember in detail the stories they once told... you can remember them with fondness.

In the case of my grandmother, that is not true.

Yes, I can recall her smiles as she put my brothers down for not being active in the craft. I can describe in detail how she would tell us how unworthy we were to be a Hound. I can even tell her wicked stories of how we are the shame of the blood in our veins.

The only love she had was for Elsie. I'd take all of the cruelty and hate upon myself rather than to have ever seen Elsie be victimized by our grandmother. I would have killed the old bat myself if she had.

Merelda Hound was a wicked woman so to hear it's her who seeks to kill the Crows and use us to do it is no surprise at all. Not for me anyway. Only thing shocking is that the bitch is still alive.

Darren left three hours ago after promising to dig deeper into this whole situation and report back in three days. Soon after he left, I suggested my brothers sleep while I take watch. They're exhausted and have been awake longer than me.

The sisters headed off to their own beds after giving us the guest bedrooms but I had to get outside. I'm not used to the indoors for so long.

In hell, it's a whole different realm with open fields and space to move about. Sure every blade of grass is dead and the trees look like they've been burnt to death but it's home. It even has its own moon. The realm is in perpetual darkness and for those in damnation there is no light, not even a star but for us guards, it's what we know.

My mind won't quiet and my body is restless, I need to move and run.

The moon is full and high, shining it's blue glow upon the woods surrounding the Crow property. The soft breeze calls to me tenderly like a mother's soft croon and the frogs of the swamp sing their midnight tune.

Deciding to run the property line, I pull my shirt off and begin to jog in my human form. I know there are no other people near this end of the swamp and no one would see me if I shifted but jogging on two legs is rejuvenating. It reminds me of being the simple man I was before everything changed.

The grass is thick but my speed allows me to cut through it like a blade. The air whooshing in and out of my lungs is damp with the fog that has rolled in but the chill in the air is invigorating. Although, nothing compares to the cool touch of Ronny's skin.

Black Bird is part of the reason I needed this run. She's a curious creature. She's fierce and her strength is a level on its own. Not just physically but the strength of her sisterly bond, her determination to create a new legacy for the Crows and to protect those she deems hers.

She may not realize it but she has claimed me as her own.

When she was in that trance she called out to me. She was trying to reassure me that she was there with me in whatever dungeon Merelda had me in. The tears she wept as she screamed my name told me everything. She is mine as much as I am hers.

I continue my run and just as I reach the edge of the swamp, I hear a flutter of wings above the treetops. Instead of stopping as I had planned, I make a U and begin my jog back towards the house.

I'm not sure if the bird above is friend or foe. Hell, I'm not even sure if it's an animal or a person and with the day I've had, this bird could be anyone.

Just as I emerge from the tree line, the giant crow comes sweeping down to me. Quickly I roll and shift.

The crow lands about fifteen feet away, an inky black mass against the grass. We stare at one another and based on the way my embers heat at the sight of her, I know the crow is Ronny and it looks like she wants to play.

Let's play. I send it to her mentally, hoping she can hear me.

She shifts into the sensual woman I've come to desire more than I thought possible.

"I've been dreaming of a good dog fight since the alley way." Lifting her tee shirt, she shows me she's unarmed though I wouldn't be worried about that anyway. Even if I were to get wounds, I heal just as quickly.

She drops her shirt and dives in the waist high grass like an Olympic swimmer going for the gold. Not knowing what she's up to, I move around before running for the place I last saw her. I don't get more than five feet when a giant black cobra shoots out from the grass and wraps tightly around my body and hind legs.

That's right, a fucking cobra. She squeezes until I feel like I can't breathe, so quickly and very lightly, I heat my body using my Hellhound's embers.

Feeling the burn, Ronny uncoils with a loud hiss but before she can slither away I bite down on her tail and yank her back.

She comes at me for a strike with her large fangs so I let go and dodge the bite but swing my paw, clipping her on the hood of her head.

We back away from one another and she shifts once more, this time becoming a large black panther. How many fucking animals can she shift into?

Her tail flicks with agitation right before she charges.

I stand on my back legs and we both go tumbling through the grass like a couple of boulders down a mountain side.

I land on my back with a heavy breath from my lungs and Ronny takes the advantage by biting down on my neck, sinking her teeth in deeply.

Gotcha. Her voice rings out clearly in my head shocking me. I didn't think she could reach me telepathically.

I think it shocks her too because we both shift immediately but Ronny doesn't lift her mouth from my skin.

"If you don't get up, Black Bird, I'm going to do things you're not ready for." I honestly don't know what the hell she can handle but I don't want to do anything she doesn't want and my cock is begging for me to handle her without care.

As if I said the opposite, Ronny begins to purr before she sinks her fangs into my neck.

Fuck!

Now, I know lore says that a vampire's bite is orgasm inducing and perhaps it is but Ronny must have kept that from happening because her bite hurts like a motherfucker. In response to the unexpected pain, I grip her hips and let my Hellhound claws come out and pierce her skin. It only pushes her further.

She throws her right leg over my waist as she pulls blood from me.

Now that she's sucking on me, a euphoria begins to fill my body and it goes straight to my hardening cock.

"Oh fuck, Ronny." Is all I'm able to get out.

It feels as if I've taken ecstasy and the way her pussy grinds against my aching dick feels salacious and carnal. I haven't been with anyone for months but even if I had just fucked a horde of Nymphs, Ronny would still make me feel like I've never had a taste of pussy before.

Needing more, I flip us over and rip my neck from her. In my haste to rip the panties from her body, Her teeth ripped my skin open. I'll heal quickly but the flare in Ronny's eyes as my blood drips down my naked chest gives me an idea.

"Take your clothes off, Black Bird." I watch as she quickly does as told and removes her shirt and panties. I stand and rip my jeans down my waist and watch as Ronny licks her bloodied lips at the sight of my cock standing hard and proud.

I reach up to my pec and cut myself deeply from chest to the V at my waist. The cut is deep and my blood flows thickly.

Ronny slowly stands, showing me her lithe body. She's got long lean legs covered in tattoos and her pussy is completely bare. Her nipples are pierced and her breasts are not very big but not small either, they're handfuls and perfect for my hands.

Ronny steps into my space and brings her cool body flush to my heated skin. The feeling is magnificent.

I put my hands on her hips and pull her harder against me to relieve the ache in my cock. Ronny wraps her hands around my neck and waits for me to lean down.

I don't hesitate, instead I do what I've only dreamt of; I kiss her.

Her lips mold to mine with simplicity and ease. I slide my tongue in her mouth and taste my blood. It adds to my arousal and the kiss which started out soft and sweet becomes a frenzy. I pull back and slide my mouth against her jaw and down her neck, tasting my blood before dipping the tip of my tongue into the two punctures I left on her neck.

Her moan has me lifting her by the back of her thighs, dropping to my knees, and sitting on my calves.

Just as she lifts up and lines the tip with her slick entrance, I let my fangs come out. As soon as she drops down onto my hard shaft, I sink my teeth into her neck once again. Immediately her pussy clamps down and orgasms.

Looks like my bite is less painful and much more fun.

I pull from her veins and drink in her delectable essence which is so much more potent with the crescendo of her release. Leaning forward, I let her neck go and hike her legs up above my neck. The angle let's my nine inches of need hit every spot in her cool pussy. The clash of temperatures is rhapsodies of heaven. The feel of her slick channel folding around my length is unlike anything in all the realms. My eyes roll back as my cock glides in and out of her tight cunt and my balls begin to stiffen with my own release on its way.

As I get to the precipice of my climax I pull her legs down and lift her up by her ass with her back still on the ground.

I slam into her three more times before I'm shooting ropes of cum into her womb with my roar flowing in the breeze. My vision blackens but I blink it away when Ronny's hair begins to float like she's submerged in water.

She blinks her eyes open and watches her black and white strands move around her head like some ethereal goddess.

I'm never letting her go and I'll kill anyone who tries to take her from me.

"I can hear you loud and clear, Drug." Ronny gives me a twisted little smile.

Fuck, now I need to figure out a mental block.

Chapter TEN

Standing under the spray of my shower head, I groan as my muscles relax. Yesterday was taxing on my mind but since my powers have come in, my body has felt different. Not in a bad way but I'm certainly not used to it.

My blood feels like energy coats every cell and hyper awareness tingles in my mind. It could be that now I have Drug in there. His consciousness seems to dance with mine, even in the silence of the mental blocks I can feel him.

After we fought and fucked in the field behind the house, I've been able to levitate. I know that sounds crazy as hell but I can!

I don't know what other abilities will pop up but levitation seems to be the main gift. Well, aside from the visions that is.

Fucking visions.

They're not about anything light hearted or fun like where the next shooting star will be or maybe what the stock market will be like in 2021. Then again, the stock market might be another scary ass vision.

Hell, I'll take any kind of vision over seeing Drug chained like an animal by his own grandmother.

I want to find this old haggard witch and end this bullshit but Darren wants us to wait. Knowing the Elders as he does, I'll listen... for now.

I didn't think I'd ever mate with someone. Finding a bond is like finding a human without an ounce of jealousy but here I am with one. Not only me though, my sisters as well.

I'm not sure how they're working out or if they plan to break the bond when all this is over but I'm positive I'm keeping my poodle.

You weren't calling me a poodle last night, Black Bird.

Drug's voice echoing in my head makes me squeal and jump a foot in the shower. I throw my hands out to steady myself but my feet never touch back down on the floor.

I look around me and see that the shower head is still spraying water but the drops from the floor are rising like gravity no longer exists for them. I don't know how I'm doing this and I need to figure it out so I can utilize it while bounty hunting.

As quickly as the thought arises, my mood drops. I can't work for the Elders anymore, not with the knowledge I now have.

Fucking bastards.

Suddenly my feet land on the floor and the drops of water splash in the tub.

I wonder if it works like the Hellfire. A chaotic mind equals a chaotic flame so maybe a light mind controls my levitation. Deciding to practice later, I build a brick wall in my mind, tossing mortar and stones up like a border wall but Drug's laugh telling me my wall is crumbling with this bond.

I smile to myself, a devious plan forming. I grab the coffee bean body wash and pour a bit in my hand, rubbing them together to make suds.

Pay close attention, pup. I'm pretty sure our telepathy works the same as my sisters only without the block.

I look down my body and watch my soapy hands rub along my breasts. I trace my nipples before pinching and pulling on the barbells through them.

Oh, Black Bird, You're playing a dangerous game.

I bite back my chuckle and replace it with a moan. I'm not much of a nipple girl, not with my own hands at least but Drug doesn't need to know that.

I leave my right breast and drag my hand down my body and straight to my pussy. Self-pleasure is not something I do often with my fingers but thinking of Drug's hard cock impaling me repeatedly has my pussy throbbing. When my fingers drag over my sensitive nub, my moan is real.

Drug's growl reverberates in my head but I continue rubbing circles around my swollen clit. I open my eyes and slide the door to the shower open and directly in front of me is a wall of mirrors.

Knowing Drug is seeing what I see, I purposely watch myself spread my folds and flick my clit before sliding two fingers into my trembling channel.

Harder, Black. Fuck yourself harder like my dick did last night. Bruise your thighs with your knuckles.

Oh fuck, this is not going as I had planned. I had hoped he'd get a boner and stab his cold brother by accident, not turn myself into a panting bitch in heat.

Nonetheless, I do as he says and lift my leg up on the soap holder before pumping my fingers fast and hard but I need more.

I drop my head back and look up at the ceiling.

Look at the mirror, Black. I want to see.

Instead of replying or doing as he demanded, I reach out of the shower and open the drawer under the sink. Inside is my favorite toy, a crystal dildo.

I look back at the mirror and lick the tip like I want to do to Drug's delicious dick and listen to him groan but suddenly I see an image clear as day in my head. He's standing in my bedroom just outside my restroom door.

It's not a future vision because I can still see myself in the mirror but Drug is sending me an image of his hand pumping himself.

I guess my plan worked a little.

I rub myself with the dildo before pushing it deep inside. I match my pumps to Drug's, twisting and wiggling it to hit my g-spot.

I'm close, Drug.

The door opens and my beast comes in, kicking it shut behind him. His hand is wrapped around his length, pumping it while watching me. He steps into the shower, uncaring of his clothes getting soaked.

I continue to fuck myself as he leans down and presses his lips to mine, tangling his tongue to mine with abandon.

I pull the crystal out and let it drop to the tiles just as Drug grabs my leg off the wall. He pulls me up to match his height and slams his swollen cock deep into me. I scream as he hits the end of my channel and he swallows down my voice.

Up against the wall, Drug pounds my pussy and all too soon I'm skydiving off the cliff of ecstasy with him on my heels.

Laying his forehead against mine, we breathe each other's exhales.

"I'm going to work on blocking out your teasing, Ronny. I'm pretty sure your sister saw my boner when I ran up here."

I want to laugh and hiss at the same time. No one sees his dick but me, but at least I threw him off his game for a moment.

"Now you need to leave so I can finish up my shower." I push his chest but he doesn't move.

"I think I'll stay and you can scrub my back for me."

Is he for real?

"I know you come from a century of docile women and barbaric men but I will not be scrubbing your furry ass. I will not be cooking like a domestic woman and I will not be cleaning up after you. I'm a strong independent woman who will literally neuter you if you try and bend me to your will. Got it, pup?"

I turn around and grab a loofa and hand it to him, "Scrub my back."

I crack up at his huff of annoyance before he actually begins scrubbing my back. Seems you *can* teach an old dog new tricks.

"I will be bending you to my will, Black. You watch and see." His whisper meets my ear before his teeth sink into my neck.

Oh fuck, here we go again.

Later that night, Darren arrives with a bag of books.

"Dare Bear! Did you get me what I asked for?" Roxy yells with delight as she bounds down the stairs with Joker in tow. I've learned the brother's names but I like the ones I've pinned them with.

"No, Rox. I did not get you a virgin nun, you'll just have to drink blood from... wherever you get your blood from."

What. The. Fuck?

"You wanted to drink from a fucking nun, Roxy?" Rory asks as everyone but Joker looks at her like she's insane.

"Of course not! I just wanted to see how long it would take to corrupt her."

I don't know why I'm surprised. Roxy is always looking for some nonsensical way of having fun. I use the word *fun* very fucking loosely.

"Anyway," Darren says pulling old leather bound books from the duffle bag, "there are very few books that can teach magic but they're all for witchlings. I figured we can use these to tap into or help pull your magic forward."

Drug sits next to me and lifts one of the books from the table, sniffing at it like a weirdo.

"It smells like Hound magic, Darren. Where did you get these?" Drug asks, tossing the book down like it burned his hand.

"Relax, I had a trusted friend block any tracking spells on them. If Merelda were to tap into any of these her spell would tell her they are sitting in her library still. She has a whole wing in Elder's mansion dedicated to books, I doubt she'll notice these are gone anyway."

Darren pulls out the last of five books and lays it on the table. Rory and Roxy come to sit on the other side of me while Stoneface and Joker stand behind the couch.

"This book is dated to your century, Drug. It talks about a special race that is part witch. If I had seen this a month ago I would have thought it was speaking of the Hound brothers turned Hellhounds but it's not."

Darren opens the book and turns to a specific page. The words are in a different language, one I don't know how to read. French perhaps?

"Right here it describes the curse that was used to turn William and his followers into the originals but it continues on to a prophecy. 'Woe to the head of Hounds for past present and future come forth seeking their fleshy pounds.'"

The fuck?

"Right, and that means?" Rory asks in full on detective mode.

Darren stands and begins pacing back and forth. "It means that you three Crows are the consequence to Merelda's curse."

Draven or Stoneface, stands in front of Darren, stopping him from pacing, "What you do mean? Our mother and father dying were the consequence of theCrow curse. Our grandmother saved us by binding our souls to our hounds."

Darren shakes his head and steps around Draven.

"If you continue in the book, the writer tells in detail that Merelda deliberately killed her son and his wife so that she could use their blood *after* she cast your souls to your dogs. Her actions were planned out, boys. Her vengeance was more to her than any of you or the prophecy."

Darren stops his pacing as he looks at us with mixtures of emotions in his eyes. Rage and avengement being the most prominent ones.

"I think Merelda has been killing every descendant of William Crow since the curse in order to save herself from the prophecy. The only reason she hasn't killed you three is because you have been considered my adoptive daughters for decades; too many questions will be asked if you disappeared. Perhaps this is why she released her grandsons from Hell, to do her dirty deeds while keeping her hands clean."

The brothers sit stoically, rage and hate marring their features until Draven shifts with a roar and bolts out the open French doors.

"Dray!" Rory shouts before she runs for the Hellhound.

Fucking hell, this old ass bitch keeps on giving.

Chapter
ELEVEN
DRUG HOUND

Darren continues to speak but my mind is far away... centuries ago to be exact.

My wicked-ass grandmother killed my parents. Everything I've known has been a lie. I remember the day we couldn't find Elsie. Unfortunately, I remember it clearly. Every fucked up detail is burned into the memory of my brain. My mother's screams, my father's howls. I remember holding my brothers as I broke apart.

I even remember when my grandmother dragged us away from the village square telling us a spell would be cast in order to bring Elsie back. All she needed from us were special ingredients from the woods. Crows.

Without hesitation and through the pain, my brothers and I grabbed our nets and went hunting. Crows are carnivorous and we always had to run them off our kills so catching them wouldn't be difficult.

Using our nets we caught three and brought them back but

Merelda stopped us.

"Your mother, foolish woman, went and cast the spell but we must hurry and protect ourselves." The memory of her haggled voice is clear in my head even to this day.

"But we have the crows you said you needed. How can she cast the spell without the birds?" Drac had asked.

But Merelda wasn't hearing it. She pulled her limbered hand from the pocket of her apron and blew some sort of black powder in our faces while whispering unintelligible words.

My brothers and I soon blacked out but her final words to us before the blackness took our sight was, "Stupid boys."

Shaking myself from the memories, I focus on Drac. Out of us brothers, Drac was closest to our mother. I wouldn't say he was a momma's boy but he was always quick to do her bidding and make her special gifts like the carving of a bird he once made her. Draven carved a buck for her, antlers and all, while I carved a miniature tree with a hollow.

We all loved Mother, more than anything in this world but for Drac... this news is like losing her all over again.

"We will avenge her, brother. I promise you here and now. Merelda will suffer for our mother."

Drac's face is stoic and completely blank of any hint of the raging inferno beneath his surface but when he speaks it shows.

"Each bone will be removed from her body."

"She will need to be tried by the Elders," Darren says like his word is fucking law.

Mine and Drac's growls echo around the room in response but Ronny speaks up.

"Hell no she won't, Dar. She killed our parents and theirs, not to mention the countless True Bloods she murdered to save her hide. There's no way we can leave justice to the very people who work side-by-side with the cunt."

My embers heat at my Black Bird's words. There's no one on this planet who can understand what my brothers and I are feeling except these sisters.

"Dare Bear, if you fight us on this I will never forgive you," Roxy says as she stands and rounds the couch to Drac's side. "We're doing this with or without your help but we'll have a better chance if you're with us."

Darren drops his head for a moment before nodding. "Fine but you three girls need to work on your magic first."

He picks up one of the books and flips it open. The book is aged and looks as if it'll fall to dust if you handle it without care but Darren flips through it with ease. All of the scents in the air remind me of Merelda and I have to keep myself from tossing hellfire at them.

"This book states that the Blood Crows must have a talisman to keep their magic from becoming unpredictable. Has anything new begun to happen with you?"

Ronny blushes and clears her throat, "Uh, yeah. I think I have levitation abilities. They're chaotic though and come when I'm surprised or... when my mind is otherwise preoccupied."

She tosses a glance at me and bites her lip. I reach behind her and lightly pull on her hair. Why is she suddenly shy? Ronny doesn't really give a shit what anyone thinks.

"Oh! So when you guys are fu-"

"Stop! Don't say any other word, Roxy! I do not want to know." Darren's eyes are glowing brightly as he looks right at me.

I'm most definitely not afraid of this man but Black Bird seems to care for him so I'll indulge him. For now.

"Listen, I know that you have become bonded to my daughter but let me warn you. I know how to break a bond and if you break her heart in any fucking way, I will cut the ties and feed you to the gators. I don't give a shit if you're a hellhound, I will do it. Same for you, Drac. I will not hesitate."

My respect for this man just shot up some. He's protecting who he sees as his little girl and I can definitely respect that. Drac nods and bites back a smirk.

"Yes, sir. I understand." I'm able to cover my smile much easier. A Fairy will never be able to harm us but I wouldn't doubt he would leave us with some everlasting marks.

"Listen pops, I appreciate you getting all protective of me but I've recently learned that their hellfire doesn't harm me so if one of these puppies hurts me or my sisters, I will turn them into floor rugs myself. Now let's focus on how to control our powers."

"I'd dye your fur pink and purple, that'll really tie up my room." Roxy whispers to Drac. It only makes him smirk and throw his arm around her shoulders. She's trying to make him smile, I appreciate her for that.

"The writer of this book says the talisman will be hidden in three places. Each place will have been significant to the witch who cast the curse. In this case, Merelda. It also says that once your powers are grounded with the talisman, you three can join together… whatever that means."

Three places that are significant to her? I hated the woman so I never took the time to learn her favorite places. I can only imagine what they'd be. A cave surrounded by rotting corpses or maybe in a pit with venomous snakes as friends perhaps?

"The script is the same for all these books, who is the writer?" Black asks looking through the pages of one. They're all written in French and the movements of each letter say it's been written by one person.

"I'm not sure, they're all signed at the back with the number five."

Darren is right, they're all signed with the number. We spend the next hour going over everything in the books including the curse itself. If what we're seeing is correct, it seems werewolves are a created race as well. A witch from long before I was born cast the dark magic upon a family from ancient Russia.

The family was known as Neuri and they somehow pissed off a clan of witches. The Neuri home was cursed and forever changed but as with the Vocem Sanguinis, the Elders at the time broke the curse enough that the family and their offspring could have their human forms back and the ability to change at will.

Suddenly there's crackling in the air like electricity breaking through a barrier. Black jumps from her spot on the couch and teleports to a bookshelf by the fireplace.

"Weapons! Someone is trying to cross our wards!"

Immediately Drac shifts while Roxy and Black ready for a fight as Darren transforms into his demonic looking Fairy self and runs out the door.

"Find Draven, make sure he's on the property, I'm sure it's Merelda."

I shift and follow Darren while the girls are on my heels. Instincts beg me to tie Ronny up somewhere safe but I'd only be doing us more harm than good. Ronny is a damn good fighter and she knows what she's doing. *Having her is an asset not a hindrance.*

Fly the perimeter, Black but don't be reckless or I'll make some crow soup with your ass later. My telepathic threat to Ronny is met with a wicked little chuckle.

This little birdy needs a spanking later but right now, the whirling wind at the *front of the property has my full attention.*

Drac, Draven, the intruder is at the gate. Make sure no one is trying to break in through the back while we're focused up here.

South and west are empty. Drac's *voice is winded like he's running full sp*eed.

East is clear too. We're heading to you. Draven says as he rounds the east end of the property with a large black crow flying beside him.

Rory's crow is the same size as Ronny's but instead of black eyes, her crow has white irises. I don't have time to compare the two similar yet different familiars because a voice of my childhood screams from the front gate.

My memories did not do justice for the hair raising cackling of Merelda Hound. There's not a single voice in this realm or any other that can make your skin crawl and your teeth grind.

The wind is causing all the dirt and leaves to fly about, almost like she's creating a vortex but then everything stops. The wind stills while the leaves settle to the ground and once the dust clears, there stands Merelda.

She wears a long black robe and her hair is black with grey streaks throughout, showing signs of her true age, older than the fucking telephone. Her face and skin though show her to be young and youthful. Magical Botox no doubt.

She looks like the female version of our father which is a stain to his greatness if you ask me.

The old hag sneers at Darren and her green eyes blaze with mockery, "Did you think I wouldn't see past the weak block you put on my books, Darren Ignis? The simpleton you used paid dearly for your foolishness."

I notice the strap she has around her torso from shoulder to hip. She grabs the strap and pulls the bag off flinging it across the ward.

Still in my Hellhound form, I can smell death as the bag lands with a thud and rolls haphazardly. When it stops the flap opens and the face of a person peeks out. What the fuck!

"I tasked you, Drug! Kill the Crows and be reborn!" Merelda screams as Darren runs to the bag with a roar.

"Nooo!" Darren screams like his heart was ripped from his chest.

He runs over and opens the pouch further, exposing the decapitated head within. Whimpering, he pulls the head out and caresses the face with a mournful howl while the evil bitch cackles with glee.

I run over to Darren and wrap my arms around him as he begs this to be a nightmare. The head he's cradling is that of a woman. Through the gore I can see she was lovely with ginger hair.

Darren kisses the woman's forehead and whispers his love before laying her down on the grass. He uses the elements to open the ground and swallow his lover's head before standing up and facing the wicked old bitch.

"I will kill you, Merelda. I will do everything in my power to end your selfish life. Today you made an enemy out of the Fairies." Darren's fires burn brightly and his eyes drip liquid flames. I've never seen this emotion from him. We never got to meet this woman. She took his heart and loved him and this bitch killed her.

"You're a foolish fairy if you think you can do anything to me." Her voice makes the ground tremble but Darren is not moved at all.

"We shall see, Merelda," Darren hisses with dual voices of rage.

The witch's gaze darkens at Darren's promise but she can't hide the fear written in her features and the man's threats.

Trying to brush off Darren with false bravado, she turns to Drug and his brothers, "Stupid boys think you can protect these little Crows? They will die just as their parents have. And their parent's parents and all the generations of the True Bloods before them!" She raises her hands to the sky and with every word her voice mounts higher.

"Uh, lady, can you like... shut the fuck up for a moment?" I say with exasperation.

"For real, right? Her theatrics are lacking," Roxy says with a giggle.

"More like her voice is fucking annoying," Rory says while rubbing her ears, "Did you ever think to use magic on those vocal chords? I'm pretty sure you could at least make them match the Botox in your face."

"Silence!" Merelda yells like the entitled Elder she is.

Drug shifts and stands beside me, "No, my mate is right. Shut the fuck up. You sound like a cat that gargled rocks and glass, then drowned itself but survived. It's truly annoying. So how about I speak and you turn on your hearing aid." Drug steps closer to the gate and it makes me fucking nervous as hell.

Smoke pours from his nose as he stares at the sneering old bitch, "You forget one thing. We are the keepers of Hell and soon I will watch your skin burn from your bones while I dance amongst the flames to the melody of your screams."

Okay, that was pretty fucking dark and it totally turned me on.

I'm watching Drug's back flex with the way he rolls his head and I'm practically drooling. He's walking sex no matter the situation. I just want to reach around him and dip my hands into those jeans that hug his ass so good...

Stop it, Black Bird. This is not the time for a boner.

I should just keep going with my dirty thoughts but I don't.

"The day you were born is a day I loathe, your sister is the only one who is worthy to breathe." She screeches at Drug before looking at me. "You think that because you've somehow gotten your talons into my grandsons that you are safe?" Ensue her fucking cackling again.

Will she ever get to the point?

"You aren't safe, just as your mother wasn't safe. Do you know how she begged, how her bones snapped with each word from my mouth? You will have the same fate and your sisters will watch helpless as I carve out your abomination of a heart."

Just before her voice is done renting the air, I teleport myself behind her and bring my short sword down in an arch. Her screams pierce the air as my right sword slams hilt deep into her shoulder, cutting through the bone and tendons with brutality. Holding onto the sword's grip, I pull her back as I swing my left sword over her chest, aiming for her heart.

Before the point touches her skin, she bursts into hundreds of black moths the size of my palm.

"Get out of there, Ronny!" Drug screams as he runs for the gate.

I'm not hearing him though because I'm swinging my swords through the air at the cloud of moths. Their disgusting little wings flapping around my face and hears giving me the fucking creepy crawlies. Their fat bodies fall to the ground and turn to dust.

Drug is ten feet from the iron gate entrance when the moths all form together again creating Merelda. Even though she's bleeding from her shoulder, she has no problem cackling and moving.

She lifts her hand and weaves her fingers and suddenly I can't move. My body is trapped like a cartoon character who has been frozen by ice, only much scarier.

Drug begins to pass the threshold of the gate when suddenly he's airborne. He lands with a bone breaking thud on the ground fifty feet back while I scream his name.

"Your puppy can't save you, little oracle." She grips her fist tighter and the invisible rope around me squeezes harder. I shift into my cobra but the ropes are still coiled around me so I shift back.

If I'm going to die like this, I'm going to curse this motherfucker before I go.

"Such a shame to have to kill you. Your parents were worthless but you and your sisters could have been magnificent under my tutelage. I can smell the magic laying latent in your veins..."

She continues to circle me as she mocks me but my mind focuses on one word, *magic*. I have new abilities, granted they're not very consistent but they're there nonetheless.

I see everyone trying to break out of whatever barrier Merelda threw up but it must be something crazy because they haven't been able to break through.

Darren has ripped up the ground around it but so far he's been unable to find an opening.

Brothers get your girls back and let's throw hellfire at it as one. Drug's orders come through our mental link.

No! Stop, she can easily kill me. I'm going to throw hellfire at her from here. As soon as I'm free we port back to the house, grab the books and teleport out of here. Got it? I mentally shout my orders to Drug who I'm certain passes the message onto his brothers because they all nod.

Hold on to Darren and your men, sisters. I have an idea. When I'm free, get them to the house quickly.

I don't wait for them to reply, I keep my focus on Merelda's magically youthful face as she continues to mock how weak my mother and father were.

I bite back my anger as best I can and focus on how her eyes are the same shade of green as Drug's. Of course, his are much more captivating.

The way he watches me, even now, with admiration and appreciation. They burn bright when he's in throes of passion and battle. The way his body moves as he fights and the fierce protectiveness he has for his brothers.

I focus on him and the way he controls his Hellfire with ease. I picture it running through my veins like slow moving lava until I feel the heat in my hand. When Merelda gets closer to me, snarling in my face, I smile.

"You talk too much." I wiggle my fingers and feel the heat of Drug's flames dance along the tips. She notices the black flames and her eyes widen with unfiltered fear. She jumps back just as I flick one tiny flame in her direction with a mocking cackle of my own.

In her hast to escape the deadly element, her hold on me slips and I immediately teleport inside our barrier.

My sisters grab their men and Darren and vanish to the house while Merelda screams like a child throwing a tantrum.

Drug grabs me and slams his lips to mine for a quick but punishing kiss before turning to his grandmother, "We're far from over, old hag. Soon it'll be your head in a bag."

Then we're gone.

Once we're standing in the house, I'm bombarded with everyone yelling at me at once.

"What the hell were you thinking, Ron?"

"You could have been killed!"

"What do you think would happen to my brother if you had died?"

"You risked yourself needlessly."

"Crow soup, Black." Drug rumbles next to me.

Everyone screams and tosses their hands around in exasperation as I stand there and wait for them to chill out. I mean, yeah I could have died but the bitch threatened my sisters, I was going to let that go. Plus, I proved the bitch could be hurt with weapons and she's terrified of Hellfire! Those are useful things to know, right?

"Did she smell like onions?" Roxy's yell is last and she screams it just as everyone quiets down so it was the only thing everyone heard clearly.

We all look at her and she shrugs, "I thought we were just yelling our thoughts."

With the chaos and adrenaline still running through our systems, we all bust up laughing at the sheer craziness of it all. Roxy and Rory wrap me in hugs and toss more threats but quickly go back to whatever it was they were doing before.

"I'll keep watch, you guys pack or whatever the fuck you're going to do. We need to get the hell out of here now," Draven says stoically before passing by Rory without a second glance. She watches him for a moment before turning away and grabbing three duffels out of the hall closet.

I want to use our sister-speak and ask her but I don't know if she has built a block strong enough to keep Draven from hearing her reply to my nosy ass questions. We can block each other perfectly but I can't seem to completely block Drug, it might be the same with her and Draven.

Rory goes into mother hen mode, ordering her little chicks around, "Grab the books, Ronny. Roxy, go get every potion already made. Darren, where do we start looking for the talismans? Roxy says they're located in three separate places?"

"Yes, they are separately hidden. I don't know what they could be. You will need to split up and cover as much ground as possible. Brothers, you three will know what the talisman is when you see it and if you dig deep enough into your memories, I'm sure you can find the locations. It's your past, you will succeed."

Darren reaches into his bag and pulls out three twine necklaces. Each of the necklaces are braided like tribal bands and they have a moonstone in the center.

"Wear these at all times. If you guys get lost while separated and can't teleport to one another, rub the stone and say this chant, 'If you get lost, rub the moon. Close your eyes and I'll find you.'"

Roxy comes back in the room with a full duffle and we all hug Darren.

"We'll make her pay, Dare Bear. She will suffer for her crimes against you," Roxy says with tears in her eyes.

"I'm sorry, Darren. I wish we could have met her." Rory's whisper is heartfelt and makes Darren rub at his eyes.

I hate seeing him broken like this. He's been our father for so long and he's been so good to us, loving us like we're his blood.

"I'm going to find a Necromancer, Dar. You'll have your love back."

My sisters look at me with furrowed brows. Maybe I seem like I'm handing out false hope because Necromancers have become somewhat of a myth but they're not. I will find one and I will heal Darren's heart.

Darren nods like a parent would to a child, like he doesn't want to tell me I'm dreaming of what can never be but I vow it.

With a kiss to Darren's cheek, I turn to Drug and grab his hand. "Where to first?"

Drug looks to his brothers and nods before answering.

"Driskill Mountain."

Chapter THIRTEEN

T eleporting with Ronny's hand in mine is an odd sensation. It's like we're on a spinning top with our vertigo off balance and our sight blinded for the duration of the travel. When we land, however, there's no lasting effects and the time it took to get here was mere seconds.

Looking around the area in which we landed, I see there are hikers and joggers. Not many but enough that they should be panicking at the six people who just popped into existence.

"Do they not see us standing here?" My question is answered by a female jogger running through our bodies without a second glance.

"I have us cloaked because this place has been a public park for ages. No mortal can see or feel us."

Once the humans leave the area, Ronny and her sisters drop the cloaks.

We make our way to the scattered picnic tables and sit at one to figure out where to go next.

Everything looks so different here. In our time there were far less people and the land was wilder. The late seventeenth century was such a new beginning for the people of what was then called Louisiane. We lived in simple homes made of flat stones, logs and mud.

Looking at the visitor's building I see even that looks modern to what I grew up in.

I follow the trails with my eyes and in my mind I can picture chasing my hound as he ran through the trees after rabbits. The trees look bigger and much older but I can still see young Drac and Draven racing up the trees to see who can reach the highest.

"Drug? You okay?" Ronny asks quietly as her sisters separate items in their bags.

Her eyes are bright blue and concerned. Why?

"You were growling like a weirdo, dude." Roxy says without looking up from the pages I know she can't read. I swear, that little pink monster is Drac's doppelganger.

Ignoring her, I answer Ronny, "Yeah, I'm good. This place just brings back a shit ton of memories, things I haven't thought of for centuries."

A hiker passes by and stares at us as he passes. He stumbles when Drac barks like a rabid dog and Roxy falls into a peal of laughter. Yeah, and I'm the weirdo.

"Things certainly have changed around here but as I look around, memories start to come back to me." Draven says as he looks up at the treetops, probably remembering how many hours we spent in them waiting for small prey to wander close enough for our bows.

"Remember when we planned to hang Merelda from a branch?" Drac asks with a laugh. The memory comes back to me like a flash.

Merelda was jealous that Father helped Drac carve a bird for our mother. She took the bird and threw it into the flames of the hearth and slapped our mother.

While mother cried, Merelda screamed, 'Your worthless runts should be learning magic, not playing with toys for their craftless mother.'

Father threw her out of the house for it but it was as if a spell kept him from completely disowning her. Merelda always came back.

We planned to hang her from the tree used to carve the bird from.

"Too bad you didn't. I'd take not existing than having that horrible woman alive." Ronny's voice cuts through the dark memory.

As much as I hate Merelda and her wickedness, looking at Ronny and knowing her more and more, I can't picture life without her now. I can easily see Drac and Draven have yet to reach the same conclusion for Roxy and Rory. More so Draven.

He's never been one to want love or a partner. He took the brunt of Merelda's cruelty and perhaps it has made him the hard hearted man he is. Rory has a long road, if any, ahead of her with him.

"Were you guys born here?" Rory questions Dray.

"Yes. I can't remember the dates but it was during the French Colonial Empire in the seventeenth century. A very different time."

"Hmm, that's where the sexy accent comes from." Ronny says with an elbow to my ribs.

I chuckle at that and throw my arm over her shoulder, grabbing the book she was looking at. It feels so natural to banter with her. I can see what kind of human couple we would have made had we met long ago. Although, I can't quite picture this gothic girl in colonial clothing washing linens on a washboard. Still, she feels right by my side.

"The writer of these books was French." I bring the topic back to more important matters.

"Have you any idea what the talisman could be?"

I look through the pages and reread what Darren told us earlier but it all seems like a riddle. No real starting point aside from the fact that the items will be in a place that meant something to Merelda.

"The only passion Merelda showed was her hatred of our mother and us. She loved Elsie... or at least she was in love with the power Elsie possessed." Dray says while going over the book in his hands. His knuckles are white as he grips the old leather and I'm pretty sure he's going to destroy it. He must hear my thoughts because he loosens his fingers and passes the book to Rory.

"You're right. The places have to be significant to Elsie. Merelda midwifed for mother, perhaps that is the place we should look first." I look between everyone and see their agreement.

"No, we need to split up. Darren said three separate places. Your wicked grandma is no doubt standing around her cauldron burning sacred wood and conjuring the worms of hell to kill us." Ronny's sarcasm is funny but it's got me thinking.

"What if the talisman are the wooden carvings we did for mother? She loathed them enough. Our devotion to mother was strong enough that the wood could have absorbed the energy." I'm not sure if I'm heading in the right direction but it's the best place to start. Nature's materials like stones, crystals and wood soak up spiritual energy like sponges that's why witches use them.

"Okay, you two go search at the place Elsie was born. Drac, you and princess go to the place Elsie was... killed." Dray's hatred shows in that last word. "Pigeon and I will go search for the place Merelda cast the curse."

Ronny shoots up from her seat and jumps across the tabletop with her hand outstretched. She grips a surprised Draven by the throat and slams his back to the graveled ground.

"I don't know what your fucking problem is with my sister but I meant what I said, I will rip your fucking throat out if you continue acting like a stubborn old *mule* with her."

Draven begins to snarl but I do nothing. He is acting like an asshole and I've seen nothing but concern and kindness coming from Rory.

"Drug, get your female before I break her."

"Try it, dickface." Ronny hisses and I smile at Dray with a shrug.

"Enough! Let's go, we're wasting time." Rory says passively. She's too soft for Dray. I don't think they're going to ever work unless she can tame the beast in him.

I wrap my arm around Ronny's waist and yank her back before tossing her over my shoulder. I grab the book we were reading and shove it in the bag before pulling the strap over my other shoulder.

"Check in as often as possible. If you can't reach us telepathically use the necklaces to teleport. Any trouble during your searches, get out of there and get back to Ronny and I immediately."

Everyone nods, even the snarling Draven. He can't see her face since her head is hanging near my ass so he's staring at her ass with nothing but anger.

Cut the shit Dray. You may hate Rory but I don't hate Ronny, turn your fucking eyes now or I break your pretty face. My mental words are growled out

I don't hate Rory, shithead and your Crow's ass means fuck-all to me. Still, Draven turns nonetheless and grabs Rory's bag from her hand like he's suddenly a gentleman.

My brothers and I don't stay mad at each other long but we do fight often. Centuries together will do that. No matter what though, we'll always have each other's backs.

Be careful, Drac. Don't do anything stupid and don't let Pinky go nuts on a nun. Draven says in our heads as we all head our separate ways.

I'm not promising on that last one but we'll be alright. Dray, if you don't want Rory, I'll take her.

Draven's loud growl probably freaked out any nearby humans but at least we know he feels something for her.

"Fuck you too, dog!" Ronny shouts thinking his growl was directed at her, I guess my block is beginning to work on her.

I slap her on the ass and slide her down my body so she can walk. The sun is dropping quickly and the last thing we need is some park ranger thinking I'm dragging a helpless girl into the woods.

I look into her eyes and see the pupil is bleeding outward slowly like a deformity in her irises. I move her hair over her shoulder and see her punctures are still there loud and proud but the veins around it are blackened.

"How do you feel? Your eyes are looking a little crazy."

"I need to feed but it can wait until we get where we need to go." Ronny turns ahead and starts to walk up the trail. I shake off the worry and immediately get annoyed with myself as I walk after her. The path we're on is uneven and the trees line the path tightly so I stay behind her.

Why the fuck do I care about her fucking health? I'm for the sex and the bond but I don't want or need anything further than that. Emotions just fuck with your head and can easily get you killed. Why get tangled in its sticky ass web?

"Tell me more about yourself." Ronny's voice cuts through my thoughts and I hear the slight confusion in her words. Hating her interest in me no doubt.

That's the thing with Black and me, we're on the same page and it's relieving yet annoying as fuck.

What does a guy gotta do to just have a *fucking* relationship without the relationship? Okay, that made absolutely no sense and I'm sure Drac would even be confused by it.

Blowing out a frustrated breath, I answer her, "You need to be specific with your inquiries. What do you want to know?"

Ronny is quiet for a while, only the sounds of our feet on the gravel can be heard. Just when I think I've hurt her feelings with my assholery, which I don't care if I did, Ronny looks over her shoulder as she walks.

"What was Elsie like?"

Chapter FOURTEEN

Having my sister's name on her lips should be heartwarming. Her question should be seen as genuine curiosity and shows that she truly wants to know me... but I'm not a normal person and my sister's name on her lips sets something off inside me.

I drop the bag off my shoulder and grab her by the nape of her neck, intending to shove her chest to the nearest tree but Ronny is no weak little hummingbird.

Before I can do as I planned, she uses my hold on her as she runs up the base of the tree before kicking off and backflipping over my hand.

She lands against the trunk of the tree across the path with her feet bracing her weight and her hands gripping it behind her back. She lets out a feral hiss followed by a low groan like the fucking exorcist. Her eyes are fully black but along with the anger in her eyes there's... hurt?

"Don't speak her name!" I yell instead of allowing her to worm her way into my little bitch of a heart.

Ronny stares at me, completely still like a creepy gargoyle guarding a castle. She looks frozen as if time suddenly stopped but when I move backwards, keeping my eyes on her at all times, her head moves slowly, tracking my movements.

I lean over and pick up the bag and walk past her as she continues to perch on the tree but her sad voice creates a series of cracks in my armor and her words stab at my heart.

"I'm not William Crow, Drug but you certainly are Merelda's grandson. Let's find this fucking talisman and be rid of each other."

I ignore her, trying to act as if her words didn't beat the shit out of me. Didn't we tell Draven the same shit? Yet here I am, acting like the same barbarian. *Asshole!*

I'm about to turn back and apologize like a man but I hear the flap of her wings before she flies over my head. It would be well deserved if her crow took a shit on my head but she doesn't. *She's a classy bird.*

We walk for hours but my mind doesn't seem to notice the time passing until the temperature drops. Memories flood my mind even as I look for a place to stop.

Why am I hot then cold? Granted, I've never once had any type of connection with anyone and throughout my three hundred years of existence, I've accepted that it wasn't in the cards for me to find a mate. It's been okay with me for centuries. Now that I've found her... I don't know what the fuck I'm doing and I'm blowing it.

My heart, body and mind are on different pages. Every emotion and reaction is on opposing ends of the spectrum in my being. Every one of my embers, the coals of my soul, burn for her, beg for her. My body reacts to her as if it's known her since the beginning of life but my mind hasn't quite caught up.

The idea of a mate has never been very appealing to me but the idea of Black Bird as my soul's perfect match? I want it, yet I fear it.

Growing up, I knew my mother and father had a loving bond. Although, at that time, being naive to the supernaturals outside of witches, I didn't know there was such a supernatural bond. I simply thought my mother and father were deeply in love.

They could never stop touching one another in some way. Whether it be father's arm wrapped around mother's waist while walking side by side or mother caressing his face as he slept in his favorite chair.

Looking up at Ronny as she lazily flies, I start talking, speaking the thoughts of my troubled mind. I know she can hear me, "They were madly in love, my parents. I remember wanting that for myself one day thinking that there could be nothing greater than to have someone who knew you inside and out yet loved each and every crack and flaw." We continue on the path, making good headway even with twilight upon us.

"Nothing seemed to ever bother them; jealousy, bitterness, envy... nothing could come between their love for each other. Then grandmother showed up. At first everything was nice, Merelda was kind and attentive towards us and began to tutor us in basic healing potions and wanted to teach us more but mother forbid it."

Ronny continues flying but she speaks into my mind.

Not that I agree with your cunt bag grandma but why did your mother forbid it when it's a part of your culture?

"William Crow was on the hunt. Mother was afraid to even hum while out in the market and be accused of witchcraft. Merelda wasn't hearing it though. We loved our mother so we did as mother said and soon we were hated and loathed. Many times Merelda tried to come between mother and father but their bond was too strong and mother became pregnant with Elsie."

The path becomes engulfed in blackness as the sun kisses the horizon for the final time before dipping low. I turn off and head into the forest, stepping over fallen trees and large stones before finding a small spring. I toss the bag down and cup some of the freshwater and drink deeply. Hmm, not as fresh as it once was.

Ronny swoops low and hops over to the water on the other side as she quenches her thirst. She stays in her crow form and when she's done drinking she flaps up to a branch.

"Why don't you shift back?" I'm fairly certain she's still pissed with me, not that I blame her. Holding someone's sins on your shoulders as if they're yours to bare is unfair and I loaded her back with William's like a complete jackass.

I don't particularly like you right now, you're lucky to even be graced with my crow. What happened next?

I sigh and make a very uncomfortable pillow with the duffle at the base of a tree and stare up at the stars peeking through the treetops. The crickets serenade the birds as they fall asleep, forgetting they're the morning snacks for their hatchlings. Momentarily, the prey and hunters are at peace, giving reprieve to their daylight feuds.

"Elsie was only eight months old, Ronny, but she was everything to us. She brought light where Merelda brought darkness. She was also born with extremely strong powers. We had to keep her inside at all times or she'd expose herself and even then it was lucky we lived secluded deep in the woods because she would cause winds and fog to come in without much effort. We had no choice but to have Merelda teach her as best she could to control. Just like you would teach a baby to crawl or roll to their tummies, grandmother taught her to control her gifts."

I change the story abruptly because Elsie's story ends in tragedy and I'm sure Ronny already knows the ending.

"After my brothers and I became the Hellish creatures we are, I gave up on having what my mother and father had. In the underworld, bonds are spoken of and rumored about but no one down there has ever had one. Maybe it's because they're not topside often enough to find their mates. Whatever the case is, it's been centuries since I've thought of that love so forgive me when I fuck things up."

Ronny drops from the tree and shifts as she lands on the bed of dead leaves below.

"It's a good thing we don't have love then."

Ronny jumps over the little stream and slinks over to me like a cat would. She drops down next to me, laying her head beside mine.

I know she doesn't sleep and while I do, I can last about three days without tiring. There's a lot of things I've noticed about our abilities that are similar. Like when I shift from human to Hellhound, I can retain the clothing I had on. Same with Ronny and yet she and her sisters didn't realize that required inner magic.

We watch the stars move across the sky in comfortable silence, listening to the occasional critter scurrying about. Ronny is supposed to be my enemy, a foe I'm supposed to hate and loathe but in truth... Ronny feels like a part of me. Perhaps if we were humans, I'd be trying to woo her and court her. Take her on dates and introduce her to my parents.

The thought hits me hard.

We can't do that. I am a guard in the underworld and Ronny is a vampire in the human world. How cruel it is to find your other half and have no future together. What will happen when this is all over? When Merelda is dead and gone, will we sever the bond?

I want to keep Ronny. I do. I want her body, her hands, her mind, her strength... I need it all. I turn my head and open myself up to a kill only she can take.

"I want you so bad. Every inch of your sinfulness, every ounce of your poison, every one of your screams... I want it all, Black Bird, and it fucking scares me. The future holds nothing in stone."

Her breathing is halted as if she's holding it but then she turns away from the stars and looks into my eyes, peering into my soul. I let her see the confusion and need deep in them too. I won't hide my fears, not if she's my mate. Secrets don't belong in a bond as ours. Maybe my honesty is premature but it is what it motherfucking is.

"I live for today, Drug. Let the future worry about the future because there is none if today isn't first and foremost in a person's life. Looking ahead and looking back leaves you blind to the now. Ghosts and what ifs keep you from what's right in front of you. I may not be the most moral person in all the realms and I might be the most venomous of all," Ronny sit up a little, leaning on her elbow as she smiles at me, showing her leaking fangs and it gets me rock hard in an instant, "but this bond has shown me that loyalty is beyond your blood. Devotion is deeper than familial ties and those two things I have seen in your eyes when you look at me. I hope you know, I'd kill for you."

I pull her over my hips and use my hellhound magic to force out my claws. Slowly I cut her black leggings straight down the middle and rip the stitch with ease. No panties to be found and I groan as I push my hard length, still covered by my jeans, against her bare pussy. With her pants looking more like thigh high boots I look up at her fully black eyes.

"Let me have a taste of your venom, Black Bird."

Ronny has many different hisses, Threatening, excited, pissed, but the hiss she gives me now is easily the sexiest sound I've ever heard.

"I'll give you damnation, Drug."

I pull her hips forward and let her ride my face.

Chapter FIFTEE

After a long and oh so *hard* session of damnation, Drug fell asleep soundly.

I need to feed but being with Drug seems to quell the hunger and I'm not just talking about the sex but just being near him seems to keep the hunger for blood at bay. Maybe it's another bond thing.

After changing into a new set of clothing I brought with us, I spent most of the night watching him sleep like a total creeper but who could blame me? He's so handsome and hard but while sleeping, he softens like an innocent human. Plus he's not a mouth-breather so that helps.

After pissing me off yesterday, I wanted to end him. I shifted because I was so tempted to see if his head was easy to remove. My crow seemed to settle my anger enough that I actually listened to his story.

It was tragic and also one of the most authentic moments I've ever seen from him. Not that Drug isn't real but normally he's closed off or quick to cover his true feelings with a sly smirk.

His story touched me deeply, it resonated with my own. Of course until recently I had no idea his grandmother was the cause of my sisters and I growing up parentless but the wicked old bag killed both of our parents. Knowing that the bitterness I held for ages was for naught helped me to feel lighter.

Sort of.

You see, the concept of love was blanketed in my resentment that even my parents didn't love us enough to stay with us. I grew up thinking love is as weak as an ice cube in one's hand. Solid and strong until the heat melts it to nothingness.

The thought that we were unlovable and unwanted built a barrier around my mind and heart. I was unwilling to ever give into the foolishness of love.

Now though? Knowing that my parents didn't leave us but were killed has lifted that boulder of animosity from my shoulders and crumbled the wall of indignation I built around my heart. Am I saying that Drug is suddenly my everything? No, I'm not quite there yet but he is my mate and I do like him and what he can do with his sinful body.

I want him like nothing else but that doesn't mean I will keep him if he can't be my partner and trust me as he would himself. The moronic tantrum he had yesterday shows he has issues he needs to work out before we can decide on this bond and if he doesn't tighten that shit up, I will have the bond severed... no matter the pain it would cause.

Why? Because this bitch don't play.

Shaking my head, I pull my phone from the duffle pocket. I don't often use human devices but I do like these little gadgets. I've watched mankind throughout history and I enjoy seeing the success they accomplish despite the fact that most humans hardly have long lasting appreciation for such gifts.

Swiping the phone, I open the dark web app I have and log into my dark account, RonnyCrow2020. Yes, I even have social media apps like TikTok, all under my own name. After all, what can a mere mortal do to me?

This time though, I'm logging on to check for a new fight I've been waiting on. That's right, I love me some brutal underground fighting. Shocking, I know.

I have many interests and fighting is one of them. Sometimes I watch the supernatural fights and I love those like nothing else but watching humans with their finite abilities rise to the top without supernatural gifts is fucking amazing.

This feed is from New York, a ring I'm desperate to visit. Barbarity is hella brutal and run by friends of Mayfly, though I doubt the Italian Mafia knows he's a supernatural being.

I'm watching the sexiest human man I've ever seen take on the King of the ring. I think I hear the crowd calling him Nico the Cold, Twitch and him are head to head but suddenly the phone is ripped from my hand.

"What's got you groaning like a wanton woman?" Drug's deep voice sends shivers all over my body but I hide it. No need to give him a big ego.

"Sexy men fighting," I tell him unashamed. Secrets are pesky little black spots that'll grow into vines that keep couples from blooming and I have no plans to become a liar. It's best he knows he's not the only one I find breathtaking even though he's number one on my list.

Is it okay that I kind of want him to be a little possessive and jealous? Probably but I don't care.

"Sexy? The only *sexy* I see are the two women in their corners."

Hissing I take the phone back and click it off while Drug barks out laughter. Asshole. I shove things into the bag, including my shredded leggings. Drug is lucky he's so damn good and brings me to heights even I can't reach on my own otherwise I'd rip his talented tongue out right now.

Hm, I guess I'm the jealous one.

"Come on, the sun is almost out and we need to get moving." Drug gets to his feet and holds a hand out to me. How sweet.

I take his hand and pull myself up while yanking him down to the ground once more. Ha! That's what he gets and now I'm the one laughing like a maniac.

This is fun, something I usually only have with Rory and Rox. It's refreshing to banter and fool around with Drug, even when he's frustrating me with his teasing jokes.

Drug stands once again and slaps me on the ass hard enough to scare the rising birds in their nests. We watch them scatter and flap away but something catches my attention. On one of the branches of the tree directly in front of us is a large black moth.

Any other time I'd think nothing of nature's creature hanging around in the woods but Merelda uses moths as her familiar. Disgusting little demons.

"Do you see that?" I ask without taking my eyes off the offending little creature.

"Yeah," is all he says before throwing a palm size ball of black flame. It sails to the moth quickly, not giving it a chance to fly away.

The moth turns to dust and as it falls to the ground, the ash floats to the east without the help of wind. Yeah that was definitely Merelda.

"What a fucking creep! She watched us! That motherfucking sadistic voyeur watched her grandson like a nasty ass bitch. I will cut her eyes out." I'm simultaneously sick and angry.

Drug continues to stand there, molten lava for eyes as he stares at the branch. I put my hand on his arm but before I teleport us away, I feel my head spinning.

Another vision is coming to me and it's strong. Not as crippling as the last one but the effects are still strong as hell. Damn I hope we find these talisman soon because I need to hone in this gift before it comes on at the wrong time.

When the world stops spinning, I'm standing in front of... me? Damn, I look good in those shorts. I never realized I got a nice booty going on. Okay, definitely not the time to be admiring myself.

Future me is standing on the edge of a fifty foot drop and below is a fast flowing river but it's not the river she's watching. She looks nervous as hell and ready to jump into action at any moment.

"Oh shit!" Drug's scream catches me off guard and makes me jump like a cat in water. It's then I realize I'm still holding his arm. I turn and look at him and he's watching future me reach down and tug on a hand until future Drug is pulled up from the side of the cliff.

"Got it!" Future Drug shouts winded as he holds up whatever he climbed down the cliff for. Future Ronny smiles at him and reaches for the object which looks to be a wooden carving of a tree. It's broken and aged. It looks like the delicate branches that were carved long ago have been broken, making it look like a gnarly wand.

As soon as future Ronny's fingers touch the wood, the ground shakes like a tremble from an earthquake. The spot future Drug is standing on breaks and he begins to fall off the cliff while future Ronny and I scream.

The vision begins to leave without the spinning or light headed feeling and quickly we're standing in the same spot we started out in.

Quickly I turn to Drug, fearing I left him behind... can I do that?

"Oh snap! I'm sorry!" In my fear, my nails pierced through Drug's bicep. I pull away and wait for him to say something, maybe curse this entire mission and leave me because it seems that in two visions, Drug usually ends up hurt. Instead he chuckles.

He fucking chuckles until it turns into full on belly laughs. I can't hold back my laughter either so I turn and begin walking.

Even though his laugh sends a warm feeling through my body and does curious things to my heart, I still yell over my shoulder above his contagious sounds.

"I'm glad you find this all hilarious."

I hear his feet crunching gravel as he jogs to my side. The smell of his tantalizing blood makes my mouth water so much that I wipe my chin to make sure I didn't drool. I can feed from him but it's not nourishment. It's a sexual thing and it might be what tightens our bond but it doesn't sustain my hunger at all.

"I don't find the situation funny, Black. Your fear for my well-being though, that's cute and I'm laughing for two very funny reasons. One; you let your panic freeze you so badly that you didn't think to just jump with me and teleport us back up. Two; it'll take much more than a fall off a cliff to kill me." The asshole chuckles again.

"Hm, but you can be killed. Good to know." I give him a sassy wink which makes his ridiculous chuckles die off quickly.

N ow that we know where we need to go and what we're looking for, we teleport to the cliff we saw in Ronny's vision.

Questioning how I was able to witness the vision alongside her is unnecessary especially when we don't know how her abilities even work to begin with. I'm certain it's the same as teleporting with her, all I need is her touch to be able to siphon with her.

I checked in on my brothers last night before falling asleep and they seem to be making progress in their individual missions. Draven still sounds grumpy as hell but Drac sounds different. I can't quite pinpoint why he sounds different but I'm sure it has something to do with his pink crow.

Both of them have seen the moths as well. It seems Merelda is watching but not attacking. Maybe it's because we're all separated? I'm not really sure but I'm on high alert.

The cliff is a steep drop but again, it won't kill me.

"Okay, Black Bird. This is the spot. Let's have a look around and see what we're working with. Whatever happens, don't touch the talisman until we contact Darren. Maybe he'll have more information for us."

I toss the duffle bag ten feet back and remove my shirt. My embers burn strongly at Ronny's heated gaze as she blatantly stares at me. I feel like doing something stupid, like flexing or something else as equally as embarrassing.

"Don't start strutting like a peacock, Drug." Ronny says with an eye roll.

I swear this girl is begging for a spanking.

Scoffing, I walk to the edge of the cliff and see there's only one path down, this must be where I was climbing. I look around and spot where Ronny and I stood before the cliff broke off and can clearly see the dry crack in the ground.

"If we tried altering the future by me teleporting down instead of you climbing, maybe we can avoid the earthquake?"

I think about it for a moment, imagining every outcome but none of that will work because it was her touch that caused the earth to tremble.

"No, I'll climb down. Nothing happened during the climb anyway."

Squatting I grip the point of a large boulder in the ground and brace myself as I swing my legs over the edge and begin my descent. There are a few good handholds along the wall but I'm not sure which way to go... left or right.

Deciding to go right, I see a huge black moth off to the side. It's too far for me to be able to smash the fucker and throwing a flame is almost impossible in the position I'm in so I settle for throwing the finger. Fucking despicable woman.

A little further down I go, until I see the corner of a box sticking out from a crack in the dirt and rock wall. Awkwardly gripping it between my fingers and thumb, I try to pull it free but my fingers keep slipping. I let go and reposition my feet and left hand to brace myself better.

With my right hand pulled back, I swing my fist forward and punch the wall with as much force as I can put into it.

"Be careful, Drug!" Ronny chastises me from the top. Her tears are probably the cutest things about her. They're endearing but wholly unnecessary.

The rock cracks and crumbles with my strength. I blow the dust from the box and see that I can grip it much easier. Finally, I'm able to pull on the box but the wood is aged and the side breaks off before I can pull it free from its place in the cliff wall.

I look into the box and see the carving I made for my mother ages ago.

With the talisman in my hand I climb back up with ease. Ronny helps pull me over the edge with her grip on my forearm, carefully avoiding the statue in my hand.

Knowing the cliff can easily break, we move back toward the duffle.

The wood is brittle in my hand but the memories are as strong as ever.

"My mother loved this gift," I say softly as I turn it in my fingers. It's six inches long and the twine my mother tied around it is still there but the branches I created are broken and most are missing.

"I'm sure she did. I can see it was a beautiful creation and any handmade gift is made with love. She must have been a wonderful woman, Drug."

That makes me smile, "Yeah, she was..." my words are cut off when the black moth I forgot about flies right at my face making some fucked up noise like an angry bird screeching.

I swing my hands to fight off its attack. It's a huge mistake because Ronny does the same and our arms collide. The sculpture falls from my hands and Ronny catches it on reflex.

The ground shakes violently and the cliff's edge breaks off, falling to the river below but leaving us safe up here.

Still though, I grab onto Ronny and see that her eyes are white while her hair floats around her face. Her hand is still holding the sculpture tightly but I can't get her out of her trance so I scoop her up and grab the duffle just before the next piece of the cliff crumbles. I continue running with Ronny over my shoulder as the ground shakes beneath my feet.

Black Bird, are you okay? Speak to me. My worry is evident in my mind as I try to reach her mentally but it's no use because it's as if there's a giant storm in her mind and the winds are keeping me out.

Dray, Drac, if you find the talisman, do not let your mates touch it. Not until we have Darren with us. Be on the watch for Merelda's moths.

Their voices come through and confirm they've heard me but even their voices are disrupted and difficult to hear. Like a radio losing its connection. What the hell is happening?

The earth continues to rumble but loses its fierce shaking quickly. I find an open field and stop, laying Ronny down on the grass. Her lips are moving rapidly but no sound comes out. I brush her hair from her face and watch her eyes switch back and forth from white to blue to black.

"Shhh, Black, I'm right here. I'm not leaving." I tell her as I keep watch over her beautiful face and growl when I see her face morph into a look of fear. I hate this! I fucking hate the useless feeling running through me. I can't reach her or my brothers mentally and I need them here now.

I grab the phone she had with her and try to unlock it but somehow hit the camera instead. Growling, I toss it aside not willing to waste a second on it. Then I remember the necklace! It's around her neck.

I hold her arm and rub the moonstone, whispering the chant Darren told us but nothing happens. Sitting alone in the fucking field with Ronny in this paralyzing trance wondering what the hell to do is absolutely torturous

Suddenly there's a crackling in the air and the wind kicks up wildly, throwing pebbles and dirt everywhere. I shift immediately knowing it's none other than Merelda but instead of the old bitch stepping through her portal, a young girl comes forward.

I growl, I will not be fooled by Merelda's trickery.

"Drug! You have to run! Take Ronny and run now! Grandmother is coming!" The girl screams as she looks over her shoulder into the portal as if someone is right on her heels.

I shift back and try to grab Ronny but the girl's scream pierces the air and her body is jolted back through the portal right before Merelda steps through. Before I can shift back and fight, something like a smoke bomb lands near my feet and the substance spilling into the air chokes my human form.

I try to shift but I can't and the last thing I think of before the blackness takes over is kissing Ronny one last time.

Chapter SEVENTEEN

"Argh!" I wake on a groan that sounds similar to a pirate.

What the fuck happened to me? Did I take too much Insania and go fucking nuts or something? Damn, I wonder if Rory had to knock me out like we did with Roxy. How the fuck do humans wake from sleep because this shit hurts like hell.

I open my eyes and the light of the sun burns my eyes like nothing else. The searing pain causes another pirate groan to escape. I roll over and try to get my bearings but the grass meets my fingers.

The fuck?

I crack my eyes open and see the carving Drug did and immediately the memories slam into me like a baseball bat to the head.

The sculpture was falling and I caught it- a knee jerk reaction- and suddenly, I was standing in a whirlwind of every possible future. It was like I could see how the world could become all depending on choices and paths people chose in that moment. I could see the supernatural flourishing but also falling. I saw the human world end with choices the people made but I also saw sweet salvation if they made the correct ones!

So many outcomes with so many paths.

"Drug!" I scream looking around for him, "Drug, please!"

I know he's gone, I know it because my soul feels the separation but also because his face was prominent throughout the bombardment I suffered... How long ago?

I grab my phone and suck in a deep breath, it's noon, it's been hours since I touched the sculpture.

What happened after that? Fucking hell. I need my sisters.

Rory, I need help. Drug is missing and he's been gone for hours.

Nothing. Not a flicker of anything from her.

Roxy?

"Fuck!" my scream is loud and scares the birds in the trees but I don't care. Everything in me is rebelling against the distance Drug's absence creates. Not hearing my sisters or feeling them in my mind is torture as well. I swipe open the phone and curse myself for the carelessness of my actions when I grabbed the sculpture.

When the screen opens, I see it was on the camera which is fucking odd as hell. I'm about to close it but decide to click into the photos and see there's a ten minute video on there.

"Drug! You have to run! Take Ronny and run now! Grandmother is coming!"

A little girl's voice can be clearly heard even though the camera is obviously on the ground recording the sky.

B L O O D   C R O W

I hear Drug as he huffs and kicks the camera like he was about to lift me off the ground but then the little girl screams bloody murder before smoke wafts above the camera lens.

There's a loud thud and I hold my breath watching and hoping for Drug's voice but my hopes are crushed as footsteps through the grass stop near the phone, "Stupid boy..."

Merelda's horrendous voice is cut off when there's a scuffle and a child's grunt of pain alongside the witch's screech of anger, "You rabid little girl! I never should have let you out of your cage!"

"Don't hurt her!" The little girl screams as the wind begins to kick up before suddenly stopping after a loud slap, like a backhand to the face.

She fucking slapped that kid! I will cut off her fucking hands and slap her with them! I'll do much more than that but slapping a child... I'll keep Merelda alive for decades while torturing her.

"I won't kill her, dear Elsie. I need her sisters to be alongside her. For now the little birdy lives. Now open the portal so we can get your mutt of a brother back to the caves."

Quickly, I close the phone and stuff everything back in the bag including the sculpture. I need to find my sisters and find Drug... and his very alive baby sister.

"Corvos copulare." *Join the Crows.*

Nothing happens but before I throw a tantrum I remember the necklace.

Closing my eyes and picturing Rory in my mind, I rub the stone as I speak the chant, "If you get lost, rub the moon. Close your eyes and I'll find you."

Immediately, I'm siphoned to a river's edge.

129

Rory is laying down with her eyes clouded over as Draven screams her name over her face.

"Dray! What the hell is happening?!"

Draven snarls as I drop across from him on the other side of Rory's side. Her lips are moving but it's the wild lightning that's capturing my attention. It's striking close to the ground.

"Rory! Come back, sister!" I scream at her while Draven cups her face while rubbing soothing circles on her cheeks. His eyes are bright with his worry and fear.

I look around again, making sure Merelda isn't trying to portal here as well.

"Dray, we need to get away from the water, the lightning is going to strike it and we're too close! Hold onto my hand."

He grabs onto my right arm as I rub the moonstone once again, picturing Roxy.

When my eyes open we're on the ground at the base of an old willow tree.

Drac is holding a barely conscious Roxy in the middle of burnt grass. Drac sees us but he keeps his attention on Roxy, speaking into her ear while laying kisses to her temple.

"Ronny?" Rory's grumbling voice pulls me back.

"Thank fuck!" Draven breathes out as he lifts her up and cradles her to his chest. I guess they figured their shit out or maybe this shook the shithead out of him.

"Listen, the same thing happened to me this morning but while I was in the catatonic state Rory was just in," I take a deep breath and pull out the phone, "Merelda took Drug. Not only that but there's something you need to see."

I hit play on the video and hand it to Draven before checking on Roxy. She looks a lot better than she did moments ago. I pull her into a hug and look at Drac, "You need to see the video too."

Drac kisses Rox one last time before jogging over to his brother.

"I was worried about you, Ronny. I was trying to reach you just as Drac found the wooden bird. I grabbed it from him in my excitement and fell into whatever the hell I fell into. I saw present moments throughout the realms and I saw Drug bloodied and unconscious in a cell. I saw you screaming in a field and Draven howling over Rory. I was so scared."

I reach up and wipe Roxy's face as tears fall from her eyes. It's a very rare thing to see Roxy sad or frightened so my heart is breaking even more, adding salt to the wound Drug's abduction has caused.

"I was worried about you guys too. Drug... I'm so scared for him. What if he can be killed in that dungeon?" I stop and hold back the sob that wants to break free. I can't break down, I need to stay strong and find my mate.

"Shh, Ronny. Fuck that cunt, and not in the fun way either." I crack a watery smile at that, "We're going to find that old hag and cut her open."

Drac and Draven's howls of pain and rage cut through the air and Roxy bolts straight to Drac as Draven buries his face in Rory's neck, his body shaking with his emotions.

I stand there, watching these powerful men break with the overwhelming news of their baby sister being alive and I snap. This bitch can't live any longer. How can someone as worthless as that foul beast walk this earth and breathe the same air as my sisters and our men? Hell no.

I'm a Vocem Sanguinis and I vow Merelda's death will be as brutal as a hook on a whip.

"I promise you, brothers, we will get Drug and your sister. She saved me and tried to warn Drug, I owe her a debt I can never repay but I will die trying. Darren said that once we had the talisman we'd be able to join together, right?" Draven looks at me differently, as if he sees me in a new light. I want to tell him that in this family, one always stands in place when one of our own needs to sit. When you break, I'll stand and vice versa. But I don't, I just continue on.

"I know Darren didn't know what that meant but I can feel it's meaning in my veins. Let's join hands and focus on Drug's location. I know Elsie will be there and I have a feeling Elsie's power is a conduit for Merelda's."

Draven steps forward aggressively but it's not pointed at me.

"What do you mean by a *conduit*?"

In the video, Merelda showed her hand by telling Elsie to open the portal. She showed that she isn't the one with the powers.

"I believe your little sister is Merelda's power source or at the very least, she's using little Elsie as a channel to make her own power stronger. If we get Elsie out of that bitch's grip, we will leave Merelda weak enough to be killed. Right now, we need to find their location and somehow let Drug know we're coming for him."

My heart hurts just saying his name knowing he's being brutalized like an animal.

Being without Drug is painful, in my soul and in my bones. I feel his loss like a drought in the summertime. An endless day of sun and no clouds in sight to relieve the scorch on my skin. His empty space beside me is ruthless in its agonizing mockery.

I once said love is painful and I was right. It's motherfucking painful because yeah, I love Drug. Fuck this pain. I will get him back, kill the wicked old bag of bones and then kick his ass for getting caught.

I hold my hand out to Rory but she looks a little nervous. I can't say I blame her. The talisman have put us through the ringer but Draven whispers something in her ear that soothes her.

She takes my hand with a deep breath and Roxy takes my other hand. We're all linked now and we close our eyes focusing on Drug.

Nothing happens right away but my right forearm begins to burn. It doesn't hurt but I can feel the heat as it begins to spread throughout my body.

The spinning starts and soon I'm standing in the cave once more only this time, my sisters are with me.

Drug is there, bleeding and hanging by his wrists. Lashes are all over his body, bleeding in some and blood caked in others.

He looks right at us and smiles.

You can see us? I ask him through our link.

No but I can sense you and hear you, it feels so good too. His inner voice sounds exhausted and my heart twists.

We're coming for you Drug and your brothers are with us. Do you know where you are? He drops his head in utter defeat and I can't stop the sob, even in my head.

Don't cry, Black. I'm okay, just healing very slowly. This room is made of something that dampens my abilities and these cuts aren't what hurts. She's using Elsie to keep me tamed. She locked her in a cage and threatened to drain her of her power. She did it once until Elsie passed out while screaming.

The connection starts to warp as if we're on a time limit.

We'll find you Drug. I promise and we'll get Elsie out of there too. I put as much hope as I can into my words, *I love you.*

The last thing I see before the vision drops is his head pop up with a cocky little smirk.

Chapter EIGHTEEN

Coming out of the vision was easier than it has ever been before, almost like opening your eyes from a dream... at least that's what I imagine it's like.

"Whoa! Look at your arm, Ron," Roxy exclaims.

On the spot that was burning is the image in the exact likeness of Drug's Hellhound. Four barrel nose and pointed ears, it even has two punctures on his neck showing that he's been bitten... or claimed.

"Great, now I won't be able to date with this tattoo scaring everyone off."

Roxy's mumbles are easily heard and Drac laughs, tilting his head to the side showing off a Crow on his neck. "Same here, Baby Crow."

Roxy hisses but I look at Draven, he too has a crow on his neck. I wonder if Drug got one. Oh Drug, I need him back, the fucker. I decide not to tell them what's happening to their sister. It won't do her any good if they lose their shit.

"Let's get back to the house and get Darren. We need to see if he has any more information to help us."

Draven and Drac quickly pack up their duffels as I grab mine. We join hands and siphon back to the house.

The first thing I do when we arrive is head for the storage fridge and grab as many packs of blood as possible. Mayfly has a few connections with nurses and doctors who he gets fresh human blood from. He sells the packs just as drug dealers would sell narcotics. He does this with anything supernaturals need. Even the witches.

Mayfly has his hands in many different buckets and he's someone I need to visit soon, perhaps he'll know something useful. Afterall, there's no rest for the wicked and Mayfly is one wicked bastard.

After finishing my seventh bag of blood I grab another and head back into the living room where both couples are sucking faces. Gag!

I toss the half empty bag, having lost my appetite at the very uncomfortable PDA going on.

"Uhh, can you savages do this later? We need to get Darren here and you know he'll burn something down if he sees you four fucking."

Rory rolls her eyes, "We weren't fucking, Ronny. Sheesh. Dramatic much?"

"Bitch, it was heading that way, Roxy already has her hand down Joker's pants... Roxy! Fuck, stop dude." I pinch the bridge of my nose.

She pulls her hand free and smiles at Drac who looks very pleased with himself. I swear, these four are going to make me ditch them.

"Here." I toss them bags of blood as I start organizing my man's rescue. "One of you needs to get Darren here while I go pay a visit to Mayfly."

Joker makes a surprised face, "Already going to go visit your fuck buddy? That didn't take long."

I'm on him in a minute and Roxy doesn't stop me, in fact she scoots over as I grab Joker by the throat, pushing his head back. Drac isn't holding back either, he grabs my throat in the same way, growling as I hiss.

"Your brother is the only man I want or will ever want. You speak from your ass, dog. You know nothing about my love for him." I knock his hand away and ignore the cuts his fucking claws left behind as I get an inch from his face while pulling my blade from my boot.

Roxy gives a warning groan, sounding like a feral demon but I ignore her as I put the tip of the blade at her man's groin.

"I may not be able to kill you, Drac but I can and I will cut your fucking balls from your body." To show him I mean my shit, I put pressure on the blade. His eyes flare but the sadistic asshole smiles before snapping his teeth in my face.

Fucker is psychotically perfect for Roxy.

I push off of him and slide my knife back in place.

"Now, I'm going to visit Mayfly to see if he's ever done business with Merelda. You guys find out if Darren has anything useful."

I turn to head upstairs to my room so I can change out of these filthy clothes but a heavy set of footsteps behind me have me turning back.

"Drug would never forgive me if I didn't go with you," Draven says as stoic as ever.

I cross my arms over my chest and level him with a go fuck yourself look, "I do not need a babysitter and if you're insinuating what your dickface brother just did, I will stab you."

I'm not fucking around either, Rory's mate or not, I will draw blood.

Draven smirks, "Of that I have no doubt but what you said back in the woods... We're a team now, a family. I got your back."

This softens my stance. I guess Draven isn't a stoned-face prick anymore.

"But hurry up cause I want to get back to fucking your..."

My boot to his chest doesn't knock him down as I had planned but it does stop his nasty words. Unfortunately, it makes him bust up laughing like a damn clown.

Assholes, I tell ya.

Once I finish changing and cleaning up, I turn to go down the stairs but stop myself. I want to see if I can channel my new powers on cue. I look across the room and see the hamper, hanging over the edge of it is Drug's shirt. He took it off the day we had our steamy shower.

I focus on the feel of gravity and how it holds everything down relentlessly, hugging everything to the earth. Then I picture its grip slipping from around the cotton shirt. I imagine gravity leaving one stitch at a time until it finally lets it go.

The shirt lifts off the hamper and I squeal like a piglet, happy to see that even with my excitement, the shirt continues to levitate.

I lift my hand and do a quick *come hither* motion with my fingers. The shirt flies to me so fast, it's like someone threw it. The shirt sails right to my hand leaving me breathless and filled with so much excitement.

I try it again with something solid and again, it flies right to my hand. I figured out that the faster I motion with my fingers, the faster the object flies.

I learned that the hard way when I was trying to get the bookend, a crystal ball, to come to me and it nailed me right in the mouth.

Okay, now that I pretty much have that ability down, I try for my Hellfire. If I'm going to fight Merelda, I need to learn how to call this flame fast without a struggle.

After a few minutes of trying, I can finally call the black flames to my fingers. It seems the flame is bigger when Drug is touching me though because the flames only come out of my fingertips.

"Let's go, Ronny!"

Draven yells from downstairs like an annoying brother. I knock on wood like I've seen humans do because having a pushy sibling is seriously bad luck.

Looking down at my new tattoo of Drug's Hellhound, I rub it with a smile, "I'm coming Drug."

"Ahh, my lovely Crow has come for a visit." Mayfly's smooth voice reaches my ears as we enter Club Lust.

"She isn't here for your drool, Nymph so put your tongue back in your face." Draven snarls from my side.

I swear, men with egos are just so annoying. If they pull their dicks out for measuring I'll cut them off. Hmm, seems like I have a thing for cutting dicks off.

"She brings her guard dog too, wonderful."

I hold up my hand, halting Draven's comeback.

"Enough. Draven is right, I'm not here for anything other than some information, Mayfly. I need to know if you've done any business with the witches, an elder to be exact."

Mayfly's eyes flare with interest before he nods to his bodyguards. The men usher everyone out of the private VIP section, "Right this way."

We follow the Nymph up the stairs but we don't speak until the doors are closed. Remembering the moth, I put a finger to my lips and begin looking around the small room. Can't be too careful where Merelda is concerned.

"What are you looking for, beautiful?" Mayfly says as he pours himself a drink.

"Black moths. They're the familiars of Merelda Hound."

Mayfly freezes but brushes it off quickly and if I hadn't been watching him I wouldn't have caught it. Please tell me I won't have to kill this guy.

"What do you want with the Elder?" he asks with false nonchalance.

"She took something that belongs to me and I want it back," I tell him coldly, the less details with this dude, the better. I don't want or need him having any kind of leverage over me because I will do almost anything to get Drug back.

"Mhmm." Mayfly sips his drink as he watches us from over the rim.

"Where is the other dog, your *mate*? He was very possessive last time I saw him. It seems rather peculiar that he isn't here with you considering it's *me* you're visiting with."

I hate lying so I choose to stay silent with my brow cocked. I'm giving the cunning prick ten seconds to start talking or I use my newfound gifts on him.

Lifting one finger, I begin counting and as each finger lifts, I let my pretty black flames lick on each digit.

Mayfly chokes on his drink at little as I count, "One, two, three, four..."

"Fucking hell, Crow. Put the flames away. I'll tell you what I know about Merelda but I want something in return."

Draven chuckles before pouring himself a drink and sitting back like he's enjoying the show.

"What is it you want?" I ask warily. If he asks for a blowie, I'll bite the thing off. Yep, definitely have a thing for dick removals.

Mayfly smiles salaciously and licks his lips like he's about to eat a full course meal at a five star restaurant and I'm internally groaning. I used to think Mayfly was stupid handsome and while I still do, this wicked man does nothing for my lady parts.

Draven looks like he's hoping the Nymph says something disrespectful so he can tear into him but I have an inkling that the fucking twinkle in Mayfly's eye has nothing to do with me.

"I have a feeling you'll bring me what I seek most."

The fuck?

I stare at him for a moment, waiting for the weirdo to elaborate but he waits for me to agree. This guy is nuts.

Draven's eyebrows are practically in his hairline as he holds the cup to his mouth, like the ominous response made him pause mid drink.

"Well, do we have a deal?"

"What kind of information are we talking here and what is it you seek most?"

Mayfly bellows with laughter like a maniac and I'm seriously questioning his mental stability at this moment until he opens his mouth and practically throws Drug a life preserver.

"Why, I'm offering you her location and as for what I seek... That's my business." That last part is said with the face of the deadly man he is beneath his charming exterior.

Whatever.

"Fine." I take his hand and seal the deal.

Chapter
NINETEEN
DRUG HOUND

Paralyzing the body while keeping a victim conscious of every moment you torture them is similar to suffering a fate in the belly of Hell. Letting the victim feel every tear and rip of their bodies while keeping them immobile is one of the most gruesome punishments and it takes a special person to give it.

The victim will not only feel the pain but will watch as their limbs are torn from their bodies and see their insides litter the ground but they can't do shit about it except pray for a death that won't come and scream for mercy that won't be granted.

I've seen such things happen within the gates of Hell and I'm immensely grateful I'm only a guard, yet saddened that I can't do shit about it. Honestly though, most of the victims there are some of the worst and most despicable people in all the realms.

Humans and supernaturals know the difference between right and wrong, they know the consequences of their choices but fool themselves by saying, *there is no hell, no afterlife.* Well, good for you, just do me a favor and keep your cries down when you arrive.

I on the other hand am currently suffering a similar fate only my repentance, or lack thereof, is not what put me here.

Another lash opens on my back as Merelda circles me with a sneer on her face. She's a demented motherfucker who would be perfect as the bride of the devil. Honestly, the bitch is fucking crazy.

I receive twenty lashes before the invisible whip stops. My wounds begin to stitch back together and in an hour I'll be healed once more but my abilities are weakened within the cave's stones.

Merelda cackles and my eardrums cringe at the sound.

"I'd rather take more lashes than to hear your brittle fucking vocal chords. Can you shut the hell up?" I'm weak and in excruciating pain but I won't let it show. My hands are bound with simple rope and I'm certain I could easily break them but Merelda has my little sister as bait.

That thought has my Hellhound stirring inside me. I can feel my eyes glowing but Merelda smiles wickedly, "Ah, ah, wouldn't want Elsie to suffer for your lack of control, would you?"

She rubs her hands together like the wicked witch of the west. What a cliche.

"How the hell are you an Elder, you demented old hag? Do they not see your corruption or have you put them under a spell?"

If there's one thing Merelda loves, it's bragging and I'm hoping this broad will sing like a canary and give me something useful for when I'm free. I know my Black Bird is coming and she'll bring Hell with her.

"Even better, little dog. They're all dead!" She cackles again like she just told a delightful story.

"I had them killed ages ago, when they broke the curse on the Blood Crows. Those useless, ignorant leaders felt like showing mercy to the disgusting blood drinkers so I had to teach them a lesson in mercy... or lack of!" She giggles.

I want to rip my ears off. Better yet, I want to slash her throat until her gurgles are the only sounds to reach my tired ears.

Merelda weaves her fingers through the air and my bindings fall to the floor. I wish I could attack her but I will not risk Elsie.

"How did you bring Elsie back?" I ask her as she points to the chains hanging from the stone wall.

When I woke up I remembered the little girl who tried to warn me to run. When I asked Merelda about her and with glee she told me the kid was my sister. I tried attacking the bitch then and that's when she began to squeeze the power out of my sister. Elsie's screams of pain were enough to keep me from attacking Merelda again.

Soon though, I will make Merelda scream louder and hopefully break those horrendous chords.

"Such a stupid family my worthless son created. You all fell for love and it's weakness therefore you all were easy to fool. She never died. I kept her safe until her powers could be useful to me. Blame your cunt of a mother, she's the reason you all are so weak."

I laugh loudly, not with joy, and spit on the ground.

"You claim my mother made us weak but it's you who needs us. You use Elsie because she's more powerful than you. You brought me and my brothers topside because you can't kill the Crows. You are the weak one, Merelda." I laugh at the lunacy of it all.

My back tears open again as she uses her magic to cut at my skin in her anger but it doesn't stop my mocking laughter.

Once I'm close to the chains, Merelda uses her power to lock my wrists in the cuffs and stand before me with rage written in her deceivingly youthful features.

"I tasked you, Drug. Kill the Crows and be reborn."

Whatever the fuck that means. I don't care anymore, I'm sick of her fucking voice and my body is hurting so badly that I just want to pass out.

"I worry not, the Crows are coming with the Hounds in the rear. Your threats are for naught, your end is near."

I feel something in the corner of the darkened room with us. It feels familiar and comforting. I turn, looking into the darkness just as Merelda storms from the room, her black robe flowing behind her.

The feeling gets stronger and soon, I feel her. Ronny is watching me. She's here.

You can see us? Her voice rings out in my head and I feel my neck burn with something, probably a slash closing.

No but I can sense you and hear you, it feels so good too. Hearing her beautiful voice soothes the ache in my soul. My Hellhound stirs and helps my body heal faster.

I drop my head on a groan as my body mends but the heat in my neck spreads throughout my body. It doesn't burn though it's just... strange.

Ronny's inner voice breaks with a sob and my heart squeezes tightly. Fuck making Merelda scream, I'm gonna rip her throat out for making my Bird cry.

Don't cry, Black. I'm okay, just healing very slowly. This room is made of something that dampens my abilities and these cuts aren't what hurts. She's using Elsie to keep me tamed. She locked her in a cage and threatened to drain her of her power. She did it once until Elsie passed out while screaming.

My vision is blackening like I'm on the verge of passing out. I can feel that my body is almost healed which is strange because in the hours that I've been here I haven't been able to heal this quickly.

We'll find you Drug. I promise and we'll get Elsie out of there too. I can hear the raw emotion in Ronny's voice but she has my head popping up at her next words,

I love you.

The feel of her presence is gone but the smirk on my face stays put. I knew she'd give in to my charms. Damn, I really must be suffering from blood loss if I'm here complimenting myself.

The black dots in my sight expand and soon I'm unconscious but Ronny's three word sentence plays on repeat, giving me a sense of peace and a reprieve from this hell.

Darren shows up at the club not long after the deal is made with Rory, Rox and Drac behind him. Of course, Mayfly is a wanted criminal in the supernatural world but Darren has promised to overlook it since he wants Merelda's head on a platter.

Speaking of, I make a mental note to speak to Mayfly about a necromancer for Darren's mate.

"So you're saying Merelda's cave is actually an underground tomb within the Lafayette Cemetery? Why would she desecrate witch graves for that? She is an Elder."

We wait for Mayfly to answer Darren's question but the Nymph shrugs and confuses us further.

"Is she really an Elder or has she created the illusion of being one? Think about it. When have you ever seen the Elders outside of their castle?" He looks around the room waiting for an answer from us now.

He's right, I've never seen the Elders out in the streets. They've never come to enact their rules or to make sure their bounty hunters are doing their jobs. They don't come to any of the gatherings or meetings, in fact, they only send Merelda when or if she's needed.

"That's impossible, I've spoken to the Freda, the Wolf Elder and the Fae Elder multiple times. They can't be illusions." Darren sounds unsure even as he says this.

Mayfly just shrugs, "Whatever the case may be... Merelda doesn't follow the rules. Her location is within the witches domain but her rule is a desecration... why do you think the witches have found sanctuary on the outskirts?"

"He's right Dare Bear," Mayfly scoffs at the endearment but Roxy ignores him, "I've always wondered why there was so much prejudices against Blood Crows even as they send us out to do their dirty work. It makes sense now. Merelda hates us so either she's spelled the Elders to see her side or they're not even alive and she uses their energy to make illusions."

Everyone is quiet for a moment as we absorb this new information.

"I want to open her throat and see if her vocal cords look as old as they sound." Roxy murmurs to Drac who nods vigorously, giving her one of his split smiles.

Mayfly snaps his fingers and one of his many guards comes forth with maps. Unrolling the paper, Mayfly begins to mark routes and paths through the cemetery. There are over seven hundred tombs and each one could be the entrance to Merelda's hideout.

"Do you know which tomb she uses or just a general area?" I question as the Nymph continues to make markings. On closer inspection though, I see he's not making marks, nor is he using a pen. How did I not see this?

Mayfly ignores my question as he pours a black powder around the circumference of the cemetery. Once both sides of the circle touch, he looks at me.

"No I don't and the general area is the entire cemetery. I see your Mate's mark on your arm, have you found your magic yet?"

I quickly cover my tattoo like his mentioning of it will somehow mess it up.

"Yes, we did. Why?"

"Then it's you and your sisters who will need to speak the location chant and it will need blood from your mate or one of his brothers."

Both Draven and Drac bite into their palms and let the blood flow onto the map. Right in the center before pulling back.

"We don't know the chant."

"You play toss the bones, no? It's like that. You repeat his name while picturing him. Your sisters will be your grounding."

Okay, I can do that. Taking the hands of my sisters, I take a deep breath and will my power to the surface. I picture Drug's face as I told him I loved him, I picture the cave he's in and the wounds that bled freely. I picture his lips moving against my skin and how his fingers tug on my hair. I can almost feel his lips against mine, silently repeating his name as I speak it.

Something tickles my nose and when I open my eyes, not realizing I had closed them, I see I'm levitating. I look at the my sisters whose eyes are white while they stay seated on their chairs like my levitation doesn't affect them. Hmm, they really are grounded.

I continue to chant softly and watch the blood flow from the center of the map to the west end of the cemetery until it stops at a small burial plot.

I stop chanting and drop to my seat. That was crazy and I totally want to do it again.

"Of course, she uses a tomb that's totally inconspicuous."

"Really? I would have thought the powerful witch would have chosen a tomb fit for a queen." Roxy says while tapping her chin like she's pondering the meaning of life.

"What matters is how many traps does she have for unwanted visitors?"

"Good question my dear Rory." Mayfly says as Draven flashes Hellfire in his eyes, a threat the Nymph understands clearly but smiles at nonetheless.

I'm starting to think Mayfly has a kink for threats.

"I've only known her to use one entrance and as for traps, I'm certain her wards are vicious enough to kill but she wants to kill you so I say we hand one of you lovely ladies over to her."

Draven and Drac jump to their feet immediately, smoke pouring from their flared noses as they growl at Mayfly but I stand between them and the Nymph.

"He's right. If she thinks he has caught a Crow for her and wants to make a bargain with her, she'll drop the ward for a moment to let him pass. That'll be our window into her domain. You four can go in cloaked behind us and once we're with Drug we can fight."

"You said our powers don't work in there," Draven says unconvinced of this plan.

"That's what I thought when I first had the vision but when I actually spoke to Drug this time he said his power was weakened but it was the threat to Elsie that kept him from fighting back."

Fuck, I hadn't meant to let that slip.

"Threat to Elsie!?" Drac shouts as Draven goes still as a statue.

"Yes, she is Merelda's power source but draining her of her powers hurts Elsie so in order to prevent that, Drug doesn't fight back. I didn't tell you guys before because I didn't want you going on a rampage without a plan. Now we have one."

"She's right, Dray." Rory places a comforting hand on Draven's shoulder, making him soften a little... not much though.

"Fine, Bird, but don't ever keep information from us again."

I nod sharply. What can you do? If it were my sisters in that situation, I would have killed the person withholding that from me as well.

Draven takes a seat again, "Merelda isn't stupid. She'll know Ronny is too stubborn to turn herself in willingly so how do you plan to fool her?"

Ouch. But he's right, I am too stubborn.

I hate the smug look that crosses Mayfly's face as he looks me up and down like I'm a meal, "There's a few options here, one; we have beautiful sex and you become mine then I tell the old witch that you'll do anything I say and I'd like to strike a deal with her for your pretty little head."

The guys, including Darren, growl at that while my sisters and I roll our eyes. It's not really a surprise he's using this situation to get a good fuck out of me.

"Or?" I motion with my hand for him to move on to another option.

"Or, if you want to be boring, you can just pretend you're under my spell. You'll have to make it believable or she'll see right through the charade." He licks his lips and quirks a brow at me.

Oh boy, this guy.

"That'll work brilliantly!" Roxy exclaims, "Now can we go? I'm bored and my fangs are aching for some action."

Much to her dismay, we ignore her griping.

"Make it worth it for her and offer me as well." Darren says. I'm sure he just wants to make sure I'm safe and get his pound of flesh.

"Do you want to pretend to be under my spell too or perhaps you'd really like a go at it?" There's no fucking bounds with Mayfly.

"Down, boy. Just pretend you knocked me unconscious with some poppy or something when I came to dissuade Ronny from you."

Mayfly ponders that for a moment then nods, "That'll work."

Great, now we can finally take the bitch down.

"How will we get out of there once we have Drug and Elsie? Won't the wards be back in place?" Drac asks seriously.

"We'll try and link all of our magic together to siphon out, if that doesn't work though...We'll have to kill her."

Looking around at everyone in the room, I see my family all nod in agreement. There's just too many people in here that Merelda has hurt. Her choices have become her doom. In our world, a balance must be kept. Good and bad must stay in balance or shit gets fucked up.

Mayfly traps his lovers in his spell but he gives them the pleasures they seek. A misdeed hand in hand with a good deed... if it can be called that.

When I kill, I choose someone who is an imbalance to the scales of fate.

Merelda hasn't kept to the scales though and she's weighing one side down. I plan to remedy that and seeing the sheer determination in my family, I know they have those same plans.

We'll see who gets her first.

Chapter TWENTY-ON

I'm completely regretting this ploy. Mayfly has his arm wrapped around my waist as we siphon to Merelda's tomb and I have to hold back breaking each of his caressing fingers. My hands are tied, albeit loosely, in front of me and they're clenched into hard fists.

"I'm going to break every little bone in that hand of yours, May."

All I get in return is a huff of amusement before he's yelling from outside Merelda's ward, "Merelda, dear! Come out and play, I have two little gifts for you."

We wait for a tense few moments until the tomb opens slowly. I can feel my sisters and the brothers standing close to the ward but far enough that Merelda won't feel them.

Mayfly puts his lips near my ear and whispers softly, "You better play this perfectly, beautiful. Merelda has the nose of a hound and she'll catch a lie. If I don't get what I want because you can't act, you'll owe something worth the loss."

Instead of the hiss I want to give him, I lift my bound hands to cup his smooth cheek and giggle like he just said something seductive. I've seen the addiction Mayfly causes to his lovers and I try my best to mimic the fools. I can't help the slight pinch I give him though.

Mayfly pulls his face away fast but plays it off like he's checking on Darren who is playing his part perfectly. He lays on the ground bound around his torso and wrists. He looks like a corpse ready for the garbage chute.

"What do you have here?" Merelda's voice is like a creaking door, opening for the first time in years. Annoying and begging for some baby oil. Hm, I wonder if that would help at all?

"Are your eyes going blind now? Maybe you should up the magic on that youthful spell of yours," Mayfly says easily, unworried that this crazy witch will turn him into a frog or some shit.

"You are wasting my time, Nymph. Why do you have a Crow?" Merelda is playing her Elder act and treading the waters cautiously.

"Come now, Witch. This little beauty came to me seeking help. She wanted to know your location so she could... get her mate back."

Bastard! The lying snake is a betrayer.

Before I can swing at him or get my hands free to stab the fucker, he continues speaking.

"Of course, you know I'm a scoundrel so I seduced her in her time of grief." Mayfly grabs me by the nape of the neck and licks me from jaw to temple. I can help the shiver that runs through, not of pleasure but of homicidal rage.

I bite my cheek hard enough to taste blood and I feel my nails pierce through my palms. To keep myself from Hellfiring his face off, I think of Drug and how much he needs me and of Elsie who is an innocent child. I giggle through gritted teeth like a maniac.

"You expect me to believe that this Crow who is mated to my grandson, fell for you seduction so easily?" Merelda moves closer to us but not past her wards.

Come on little old bitch. Just a little closer.

"And what of the Fairy? You think I'm a fool, Nymph? I will kill you where you stand!" Fuck, this woman her theatrics.

"Listen, I can takes these two back with me and not blink an eye. Having this fine piece of specimen as my pet is not a bad idea. The Fairy tried to talk her out of my bed but I simply used my special blend of poppy to render him unconscious." Mayfly's eyes glow purple with seriousness and deadly power, "Now, if you are finished with your show of false dominance, I'll gladly hand them over... for the right price that is."

Merelda looks hesitant like she doesn't believe I'm truly spelled by Mayfly so I do the only thing I do without throwing up.

I turn and caress the Nymph's cheek with my nose before biting his neck. I don't put any pressure but he plays it as if I just gave me the most pleasurable Vampire bite possible. Of course, I'd rather chew my own fingers off than to give to someone what only belongs to Drug so I pull back after a moment of acting. I feel dirty but again, I remind myself that I will sacrifice for those I love.

Hopefully I won't have to act too much longer.

I continue to stare at Mayfly like he's God's gift but I keep a close eye on Merelda with my peripheral. My heart leaps when she cackles and steps forward, weaving her fingers through the air like fucking Darth Vader, pulling her wards down.

As she steps away, I see the vines move at the entrance to her tomb as a breeze flows by them.

We're in! Keep the act going while we look for Drug and Elsie.

"How do I know this little slut won't attack me the moment you're out of her sight?" Merelda sneers as she looks me up and down.

I want to rip those green eyes out of her head. She doesn't deserve to have the same shade of coloring as Drug.

"Oh she'll listen because I've only just spelled her. Even without my presence, she'll be wanton for me. She'll behave if you promise her you'll bring me to her."

Mayfly looks me in the eye, "Isn't that right pet?" His voice is purred with his power, a tool used to control his submissive.

"Yesss," I hiss out softly like a drug addict begging for their next hit.

Merelda makes a non-committal sound but begins weaving a levitation spell over Darren's prone form. I gotta give it to him for not freaking out when his body lifts off the ground and begins to float towards the tomb entrance and into the darkness.

She looks at me and smiles viciously, "Come now, little slut. I have quite the show for you down in my humble abode."

God, even her sarcasm is shitty.

I turn to Mayfly when he squeezes my shoulder, he gives me a serious look, "I'll be back to visit you and collect my debt. Be a good girl and I'll make sure you are sated wonderfully."

I'm hardly paying attention to the words because he drags his fingers down my chest and slyly tucks something into my cleavage. Then he backs up before snapping his fingers and disappearing.

Merelda grabs me by the hair on the back of my head, yanking hard enough to knock me to the ground. I land on my ass and glare at the foul woman standing over me. I curl a lip at her but she kicks me in the face. She uses her magic with the blow to my face and I feel my nose crunch.

I scream in pain, having never felt a broken bone in my life. My bones begin to mend but the pain of that hurts as well. I roll over as the bitch brings her foot down with the intention to smash my face further.

The ground vibrates with her stomp. The fuck are her feet made of, bricks?

I quickly stand to my feet and smear the blood from my nose and mouth. I will fuck this bitch up! I let a warning groan out before I hiss when she steps closer. Fuck this.

Using my speed, I'm in her face in a second, bringing my forehead down on her nose as hard as I can. The world spins as her nose breaks under my headbutt but I smile when she screams. Not willing to lose the advantage, I break the ropes around my wrists and grab her by the throat before slamming her back against the tomb's stone wall.

I do this three times before she wraps her boney hands around my biceps and knees me as hard as she can... in my fucking pussy!

Listen, I know I don't have balls but any woman will tell you, a knee to the crotch hurts like a motherfucker. I don't give a shit how tough you are, it's lips and bones down there, people, and it fucking hurts.

But I don't grab myself and howl. I flip my claws out and swing my arms at her like I've lost my mind, and in a way I have. She has taken enough from me and I'm done with her. I want to watch the air leave her lungs and smile as her soul slips from her body.

My nails scratch across her chest, opening her skin with ease. I want her body to look as bad as Drug's did after she flogged him like a fucking Roman soldier would. I swing my left arm but before I make more lacerations, Merelda explodes into those nasty screaming moths.

Instead of fighting off the grotesque creatures like my mind wants to do, I run straight for the tomb before cloaking myself.

The stairs are narrow and steep but I teleport myself down to the bottom and into a rounded room with three different tunnels. I have to hurry because I can hear the wings of those fuckers getting closer. I don't want to teleport any more than I need to because there's a good chance this bitch can feel the power of a siphon like Drug did when we first met in the alley.

God, that feels like years ago when in reality it was only weeks ago.

Focusing back on which way to go, I decide to go right. Most people are creatures of habit and going right is usually what they do. Merelda is as close to a human as any supernatural can get so I'm hoping this is the correct tunnel.

There are sconces along the walls and their light allows me to see the runes written along the stones. I wonder if this is what keeps Drug's powers weakened?

I get to the end of the hall and to another set of stairs but my heart sails high when I hear the voices of my sisters.

Uncloaking myself, I run to the sounds of their whispers but stop cold in my tracks when I see Elsie holding her hands up to my family.

At her fingertips are the black flames of Hellfire.

Okay, shit just got crazy.

Merelda left quickly a few moments ago but before she left she pulled Elsie from her cage and put her before as a guard.

"Keep watch over your brother until I come back. You know the consequences of disappointing me, child."

After the bitch's footsteps fall silent, I look at Elsie. She's so beautiful and looks like the younger version of our mother. Her hair is long and black as night like father's but her eyes are lavender like our mother's. Simply stunning, my little sister.

Right now though, she looks so fearful. She holds her hands behind her back and something glows against the wall like she's holding a lit candle back there.

"What's happening, Elsie?" I try to soften my voice as much as I can but the latest whipping has taken a toll on me.

"I don't know." She folds her lips in like she's trying to keep her words back.

I stare at her a moment, wondering if I can trust her or if she has a form of Stockholm Syndrome. Although, I don't see Elsie having sympathy for the woman who regularly uses her without a single care for her.

"Are you sure you don't know or are you afraid of what Merelda will do if you tell me? I won't tell her anything and when I get out of here, my mate and I will keep you safe from the old crone."

She brings her hands forward and shows me her fingers which are all lit with Hellfire. What the fuck? How does Elsie have this ability?

"Don't speak... of Grandmother... that way." Tears leak from Elsie's eyes as she visibly struggles not to say the words.

I see. Elsie has been spelled to do Merelda's bidding. I growl at the pure evil of Merelda. The vain bitch that she is even has Elsie defending her honor.

"P-please, Drug. Don't do... an-anything."

"Okay, Elsie. Okay. I'm sorry." I hang my head and wait for her to drop her hands. When she does, the fire licks up her palms but they don't burn her. So many unanswered questions.

"You look just like our mother." I tell her after a few moments of silence. "We all knew you were going to be her twin, the splitting image of her except you have father's hair."

I hear her little hiccup of emotion but I keep talking, "When you were just a baby, Drac used to carry you around in a sack on his back. He said he wanted to teach you how to hunt so you could grow up strong and abled. Draven used to make funny faces to get you to giggle, you were the only one who could get him to smile."

I stop and control my own emotions just thinking of the normal life we once had.

"Wh-what about y-you?"

I look up at her face and see the struggle she is suffering but I don't want to add more to it by acting out in anger on her behalf.

I clear my throat before I answer, softening my voice, "I made you a wooden sword and used to pretend I was a Lord and you were a squire under my tutelage." I chuckle at the memory of tying the handle to her little chubby hand with twine.

I can see the smile she wants to let loose but Merelda's spell keeps it from coming through. Fucking bitch will pay.

I open my mouth to tell her more but the feel of the room changes like Ronny is here, unseen. Elsie feels it too and she brings her arms back up looking around in alarm.

Suddenly Draven and Drac are standing there with the sisters sans Ronny.

"Brothers! Elsie is under Merelda's influence!" I barely get the words out when Elsie flings Hellfire at them. On instinct, my brothers shield Rory and Roxy.

"Elsie, stop! Fight it, these are your brothers!"

"I-I can't!" Elsie shakes as the spell and her own will clash together. She throws more fire at the backs of her brothers.

"Mother used to sing to you about the stars and the sky, she would rub your forehead with her fingertips until you fell asleep." She continues to fight the power but lets two more flames go even as she cries out.

"Father used to toss you high into the air and catch you. Your giggles and scream of delight would scare the squirrels out of their dens, chittering as they went." Draven says as he turns around and takes a flame to the chest.

Hellfire doesn't wound us but it does hurt like a bitch when they come from someone else.

"When you would wake up at night, I would go to you and sneak you out into the woods to find the moon flowers." Drac says as he too turns around.

"I want t-to stop b-but the spell..." Elsie breathes hard and her forehead is covered in perspiration. "It's t-too strong!"

Just then, Darren comes running in, "Rigescunt Indutae!"

Elsie freezes on the spot, arms up and eyes wide.

"What did you do to her!" Drac roars and dives for Darren but Draven and Roxy stop him.

"I literally froze her. She's unharmed and the spell will wear off in five minutes so we need to move quickly!"

Drac runs to Elsie and kisses her head as Draven cups her face, "We've got you little sister. You'll be safe soon, I promise."

Roxy and Rory begin working the chains on my wrists but they're magical. They won't open with a key.

"You can't break these, take Elsie and go now before Merelda comes back!" I yell at them but the two crazies just keep trying to break the chains while Darren stands watch over Elsie and the spell he cast.

"We're not fucking leaving you, pup. Besides, Ronny is outside keeping the old crone back." Roxy says followed by a grunt when Rory elbows her.

"What the fuck!?" I snap at them, "You left your sister out there with her?"

Roxy, unapologetic as ever, just shrugs at Rory, "What? Draven said no secrets, right?"

I feel a new pulse through the room as Elsie unfreezes and launches a flame against the stone floor just as Ronny comes to a stop at the door. My breath wooshes out of me seeing she's got blood all over her face but she looks unharmed.

Either she just used her teeth to rip out Merelda's throat or she's just had a meal.

Another flame gets thrown and it hits Ronny on the chest. She screeches and claws at herself, forgetting she can't be harmed by Hellfire anymore, and a vile falls out of her cleavage.

I try not to lick my lips at the voluptuous sight of her pillowtop breasts but I'm a creature from Hell, I have no morals.

Darren yells out his spell again and Ronny scoops up the little vile from the stone floor before running straight to me. She hands off the vile and throws herself at my chest.

I can't wrap my arms around her but I do take in a deep breath, filling my lungs with her scent and soothing my aching soul. She litters kisses all over my face before coming to my lips.

The burn on my neck starts again but I ignore it as I push my tongue into Ronny's mouth, tasting her sweetness and swallowing her moans. My body heals and something begins to happen as the warmth in my neck spreads to my arms and back. The urge to hold Ronny in my arms fills my mind and every cell in my body is willing my wrists to be free. Suddenly my arms pull from the wall as chucks of the stone wall crumble around us.

We don't break the kiss though, how can someone cut this short? Having Ronny in my arms is like having my soul mended with stitches of heaven made thread. Healing and renewing.

All too soon, Ronny pulls back, "Merelda will be here any moment. We need to get Elsie out of here."

Rory sniffs the liquid in the vile, "This is Praesidium. Maybe it'll fight off Merelda's spell on little Elsie."

"It will, that is the same stuff we give you to keep spells from being used to influence your will. Quickly, give it to her."

Rory rushes behind Elsie while Drac and Draven grab hold of our sister's arms. Darren speaks the words that release her from the freeze spell and my brothers hold her arms down. Rory squeezes my sister's jaw with enough force to open it then she pours in the liquid, holding her head still while she swallows.

Elsie shakes and forces herself to drink the potion and when she does, the effects are immediate. The Hellfire leaves her fingers and she sags against Drac in relief.

"Thank you, Ronny," Elsie whispers before she passes out. She's exhausted from her fight but she won't be able to rest until we escape from this godforsaken tomb.

Suddenly there's a loud scream from the tunnel leading into the room, "Here she comes!" Ronny shouts.

"Everyone, join hands!" We all follow Rory's instructions just as Merelda comes into the room bleeding from her face and chest.

"See ya, biotch!" Roxy says before we siphon to Club Lust.

When we arrive, we all turn to Drac who holds Elsie, only, it's not the little girl we left with. In her place is a young woman who looks like our mother while wearing the too small clothes of our little sister.

"What the hell?" Roxy exclaims before sniffing the woman in her man's arms, "It's Elsie but... Older?"

"The spell Merelda had on her must have kept her old enough to channel her magic through but young enough to keep powerless. This is Elsie's true self."

Darren says with sadness. Elsie grew up mentally but never grew up physically. I rush over and cup her sweet face, if it weren't for the straight black hair, I would have thought she was Mother.

"Quickly, let's get inside, now."

Once we make it into the club, Drac lays Elsie down on a booth and she begins to wake. She sits up confused until she sees us.

"Oh, my brothers!" Her sob breaks through as she gathers us in her arms with me awkwardly hugging over her head and down her back as she continues to sit in the booth with my brothers at her sides. My baby sister is alive! She's right here in our arms and she's okay now.

I kiss her head before turning around and grabbing Ronny, "Elsie, I want to introduce you to my mate, Ronny Crow, or as I call her, Black Bird."

Elsie smiles so big and stands to hug Ronny, "I've watched Ronny since she and her sisters were born. I knew they'd be mates for my brothers. I left you a guide written in riddles so you'd be able to set my brothers free from their bindings in Hell."

"How did you leave clues?" Ronny asks before I can.

She smiles at Darren, "I wrote the books Audrey took for Darren."

Darren sucks in a breath at the name of his dead mate and I sincerely mourn for him. I can't imagine living knowing my mate was dead. I'd follow Ronny soon after if I ever lost her.

Elsie reaches over and squeezes the Fairy's hand, "Worry not, Darren, your mate will be back in three moons. She is only resting in a peaceful sleep."

Darren sags in relief and drops to the booth with a sob of joy but we all stare at Elsie in complete and utter confusion.

Ronny is first to speak, "Who are you, Elsie?"

"I am the *true,* True Witch."

Chapter TWENTY-THR[EE]

A True Witch. True motherfucking Witch!

Color me shook, bruh. That's absolutely nuts. Yes, we all thought Merelda was one but it made sense. She is an old as fuck woman who seemed to be the most powerful in all the realms. It's why she was placed in such a position of power... or was she?

"Elsie, what happened to the Elders?" I ask as Drug looks at me like he already knows and it doesn't look like it's a pretty story

"How about I tell you from the beginning?"

Her voice is strong and filled with so much wisdom even as she says the simple words. I feel like I'm in the presence of someone to be respected. Hell, I almost want to dust the seat off for her or throw my jacket down on the seat so she doesn't get dirty.

Maybe it's just because she's Drug's sister and I definitely want to be good with her... nah, it's the magic. Witches are no joke and the power rolling off her is palpable. I am not fucking with her. I'd be afraid she'd turn me into a giant hairy boar if I told her a dirty joke or some shit.

Elsie sits down with her back to the VIP area. The club is empty but I know Mayfly will be down here soon to see if I brought whatever the fuck it is he seeks most. Just as I suspect, the Nymph comes out of the room and stops dead in his tracks with his mouth going slack.

I mean, I know I'm covered in blood but damn, rude much?

Elsie begins talking so I ignore the weirdo and focus on her tale, "Obviously, I don't remember being a baby or any of the moments with you guys and our parents but for as long as I can remember, I've been with Merelda. For years, I was kept in the tomb because she said it wasn't safe for Witches. Little did I know, she was siphoning my magic." Elsie opens and closes her fists and I can imagine the feel of her power being used against her will.

That's like rape. At least in my mind it is and I will murder the old bag. I reach out and grip Elsie's hand with my own, squeezing it to let her know she's no longer a victim.

Her smile is instant and so fucking sweet that I want to hug her. She has to have some sort of enchantment allure or something cause I want to buy her a teddy bear too. The fuck?

"As the years went on, I started to notice her face and body changing from the grandmother I grew up with to the young girl you saw today but I never changed. I was twenty five and I still looked like a child. Merelda said witches grow at slow rates and one day I'd bloom but she claimed to use magic to keep her young. I suspect now," Elsie says as she looks herself over, "that she was using me in that aspect as well."

Mayfly slowly makes his way over to us but he doesn't interrupt Elsie.

"Then one day, I tried to leave the tomb. She caught me and used her influence on me. I had no idea how to use my magic. She refused to teach me because it was too dangerous, at least that's what she claimed, therefore I couldn't fight back. Once I was under her spell, she went from protective grandmother to abusive and hateful."

She stops speaking and looks down, her chin trembles but she doesn't let her sobs break through.

"Shh, Elsie, you don't have to continue." Drug coos from my side and I agree, this story can wait, she doesn't need to relive her trauma.

"No, I'm okay. I just need some water. You need to know this, the world needs to know it."

Mayfly comes to her side and hands her a glass of water and she nods her gratitude but she doesn't look up. She wipes her eyes and takes a drink before continuing, eyes cast down to the table's top.

"One day, I fought the influence enough to follow her. She met with a handsome man, a Nymph. He was very good with getting her to talk." All of our eyes jump to Mayfly who just leans against the table with a smirk.

"He made Merelda so mad when he made fun of her in one way or another. He called her an *incompetent woman* and she exploded. She boasted of killing the Elder's when they gave abilities to the Blood Crows. She said they deserved to be killed and she ran the witches off her territory when they wouldn't acknowledge her as the True Witch. She boasted of her grandsons being Hell's beasts and having the ultimate power in her grasp. Soon though, she clammed up once more and left the Nymph before he could get more out of her."

We're all quiet and absorbing her story. How in the hell did she manage to kill the Elders? That should be an impossible feat.

"How did she kill the Elders?" Rory asks kindly

Elsie shrugs, "I don't know but she would leave often to check on her *pets*, as she called them."

"Pets?" I ask in confusion.

"I'm not certain what she meant but I do know they are not furry creatures. She said they were her special made weapons."

What the hell could that mean? Did she have minions or clones? I wouldn't put it past her.

"I was never able to fight the influence again after that she caught me once more and beat me so badly that I could do nothing else but fall into her trap. Later, in one of her vain boasting sessions, she told me that my brothers were nothing but guard dogs in hell, a fate they deserved for siding with mother."

"God, this fucking broad is such a twisted bitch, isn't she?" Roxy says under breath as she wraps her arm around Drac's waist.

"She is," Elsie says. "She had our parents believe I was killed so that she could steal me away. I wrote the journals when I was older. I began to receive visions of three sisters who would be the mates to my brothers. Their souls would call out to their other half throughout the years and when the time was right, no matter where you all were, my brothers and their souls would answer the call."

Elsie smiles brightly and if this had been a week ago, I would have snorted at the hope in her voice, but now? I look at Drug and see everything I want in life. He's it for me and no matter what I do, I can't get over it.

He has my crow on his neck, he's mine and I'm his.

"I watched you Crows because Merelda said you were a curse to the Witches. You three were damnation to them and she had to kill you and your bloodline in order to protect the legacy. At that point, however, I already knew who you were and who she truly was. So I set things in motion as best I could. I made sure Darren, a devout and beloved man of power, would find you three. I knew he'd love and protect you. I also wrote the books so you'd have a way to gain your given abilities."

She looks at Rory first, "While you all have the same abilities, you will find your affinity for one over all the others. You have the gift of Fulgur, *electricity* and you are the world's oracle of the past."

To Roxy, "The gift of Gehénnam, *Hellfire,* and they only oracle of the present."

Elsie turns to me and smiles brightly, "Ronny, you have the gift of Subvolo, *levitation*, and you are the oracle of the future."

Everyone scarcely breathes as this information hits us like a ton of bricks. Yes, I knew that I and my sisters were more than just Blood Crows and we had new abilities but If I'm honest, it hadn't really struck me until this ethereal little Hound said it.

I'm telling you, she's enchanting. She could make the fucked up songs Roxy sings sound like a sweet lullaby.

I look up and see Mayfly still standing there and I remember I was supposed to keep my end of the deal.

"Mayfly, thank you for tonight but I'm afraid I didn't bring anything back. I will keep my end of the bargain though, I owe you a great debt."

Everyone, including Elsie, turns to look at the Nymph but his eyes are on Elsie.

"But you did bring me what I seek most, Crow." Elsie's sharp intake has me tense in a split second but Mayfly's words suck all the air out of the room,

"You brought me my mate."

D arren walks out of the room muttering under his breath what sounds like, *here comes the drama, no thank you,* as Drug and his brothers jump to their feet. Growls and snarls reverberating around the empty club as they surround the Nymph. Mayfly doesn't take his eyes off Elsie though even when Drug shifts and tackles him to the ground, teeth snapping in his face.

"Drug!" I yell, "Get off of him! That is your sister's mate and killing him before the bond is severed will hurt her!"

Drug shifts but doesn't move from his place. Knees on either side of Mayfly's waist with his hands pinning down the Nymph's arms, Drug harshly snaps at him, "You will not have her. You think you're good enough for my sister after fucking everything in sight? No. You're not and you never will be."

Okay, that was fucking mean as hell. I didn't even say that shit to Draven when he was being a dick to Rory. I don't really give a shit about Mayfly but Drug's words hurt Elsie. She has a blank look in her eyes like what Drug said was something Merelda has said to her multiple times and now she's falling into herself to protect her mind.

I lift my hand to Drug's back as he continues to shit talk Mayfly. I close my hand into a fist on instinct and he lifts off of the Nymph. Draven and Drac turn to me and snarl but I flip them off.

"You foolish boys," Rory says, crossing her arms over her chest and cocking a brow to Dray.

"Elsie, which one do you want me to kick first, hmm?" Roxy says with a twisted smile.

I bring Drug over to my side and drop him to his feet. He gives me a chilling glare but I smile and smack him on the back of his head.

"Listen, pup. Your stupid words hurt your sister." I point to her and watch him deflate as Elsie keeps her eyes on Mayfly.

You said shit that made her curl up inside herself. Think before you fucking speak, meathead. Merelda has verbally abused her and hearing shit like you just said is making her relive those moments.

He doesn't reply to my voice but I know he heard. His back tenses as the words register.

Tentatively, Drug places his hand on Elsie's shoulder and she snaps out of her trance-like state.

"I'm sorry, Else. I didn't mean to hurt you in any way."

"You've got three very protective brothers, Elsie, but I will prove to them I am good enough for you," Mayfly says just as the building shakes like we're about to be hit with a tornado.

"Merelda is here!" Darren yells from the front doors.

"Stay back, Elsie. Do not come out until one of us comes and gets you." Drac tells her but they all run for the door without waiting for a reply.

Fucking boys. I don't want her out there either, we just got her out of that shithole and I'll be damned if she gets taken away from us again. Still though, the Hound brothers have a lot to learn in how to treat a woman, they're suffocating her and it will eventually push her away.

I get the protectiveness but I think I'm going to have to teach them a thing or two about modern day equal rights... or cut their junk off. Yeah, I might go with that.

"This is your time to prove to *Elsie* you can and will be the best mate for her. If she wants to fight, don't be a dick and stand in her way. Stand beside her and help her through it all."

I've never seen this side of Mayfly and he's never called me anything but some sort of endearment but I know that's all done with.

"I will, Ronny." He looks at Elsie, "I swear it."

I leave the two mates and join my sisters at the door before teleporting to our men.

Just to give them a taste of his archaic attitude, I put a hand on his chest, "I got this, *flower*, stand behind me and I'll protect you."

Drug sighs with exasperation before grabbing my arm and tugging me back to his side while I chuckle.

Am I an ass who has shit timing for sarcasm? Yes, yes I am.

"What's up pussycat? Damn, you look like shit," Rory says to Merelda and its then I notice she's fucking ooooold. I'm talking dusty ass old.

Roxy begins to sing a hilarious song that perfectly fits the old lady before us, "Do your tits hang low? Do they wobble to the floor? Can you tie them in a knot? Can you tie..." Drac barks out laughter but Merelda doesn't see the cleverness.

"Where is she!?" The old bat screeches as she weaves her hands together before launching a glowing orb at Darren who dodges it just in time. It hits the pillar behind him and begins to melt the stone.

Everyone dives and jumps out the way of those flying orbs Merelda is launching in quick succession. Pretty fucking energetic for a walking corpse. But it shouldn't be a hard thing to end this bitch.

After dodging another melting goo ball, I jump to my feet and grab her in my levitation. I pick her up about ten feet before slamming her down to the ground but the bitch hops back up like a kangaroo!

She throws her hand out and something like a wooden stake shoots out of her hand before slicing across my bicep. Screaming I roll and scramble behind a nearby tree. This crazy witch just staked my arm!

My skin is opened wide and bleeding profusely but it's also stitching back together again. Thank fuck!

I jump out from my hiding spot and see Rory throwing lightning at the old crone. One strikes her in the back, making her screech so loudly that we have to cover our ears. I can feel my eardrums rupture and the pain is so fucking unbearable that I thank the curse for giving me healing abilities. A first for me.

Okay, more lightning bolts, Zeus! I shout in Rory's head.

The guys are throwing Hellfire from their mouths like dragon dogs but Merelda seems to be blocking the flames with an invisible shield. Fucking magic, I tell ya.

I teleport behind her and slam my short sword into her back causing her to screech again but this time I bring my other one across her neck, slicing through her vocals like a hot knife through butter.

I lift my booted foot off the ground and kick her in her lower back, pulling my sword free and knocking her to the ground.

I lift both of my swords up into the air, ready to kill this bitch but she rolls to her side and I see her lips moving rapidly.

Black Bird! Behind you!

Drug shouts in my head just before something slams into my back and throws me ten feet from Merelda. I shift in the air, flapping my Crow's wings so I don't hit the ground but I shift back and stand next to Drug.

Standing behind Merelda is a group of what looks like twisted and deformed monsters. I've never seen this species before. The one that hit me looks like a fucked up minotaur complete with the human body and a bull's head but waaaay more scary.

Its hooved feet are turned backward and its mouth hangs wide open but its eyes, there's something familiar about them. All of these monsters look like fucked up creatures made of different species and put together by a blind creator but they all have that familiar feel to them.

Merelda must have healed from her wounds because that annoying voice of hers rings out.

Chapter

TWENTY-FIVE

ELSIE

"**D**o you like my pets? They should feel like...*family*.
"Oh shit. The pets were Blood Crows! Their ancestors who she ripped from their lives for generations! I have to do something.

"Mayfly, did you ever acquire anything from Merelda? A precious stone would work best."

I'm still reeling from the fact that this Nymph is my mate. I've felt the call my soul put out but never did I think I'd have what it desired. Hell, I didn't think I'd ever be free of the witch and I'm still not, but I've been practicing my magic while in her tomb. Any chance I got, I tried to learn my own abilities.

If Mayfly has what I need, I can get some blood from her somehow. Maybe pretend I want to go back with her?

"Yes, I have a hexagonal Hibonite. What else do you need?" Mayfly watches me like a predator but I don't feel unsafe in his presence. In fact, next to my brothers, Mayfly makes me feel free and protected.

Shaking myself of my errant thoughts, I grab the stone from his hand and feel the vibration of its energy.

"I will need you to hand me over to Merelda. I need her blood. Just a small amount on this rock and I can take her power from her long enough to kill her."

Mayfly looks at me in a truly frightening way, but again, I'm not worried he'll hurt me.

"No, Vrăjitoare Mică, I will not risk losing you when I just found you."

Mayfly takes the stone from my hand and runs to the doors before he looks back at me. I'm right on his heels though, so as he turns back our chests meet harshly. Mayfly wraps his arms around me quickly and leans in making my breath quicken and my blood pump with pure lust.

He places his lips oh so close to mine but doesn't kiss me, "I will get you your blood but I need you to pretend to hand me over for tricking her."

Then he rubs his nose from the corner of my mouth to my forehead, inhaling as he goes before placing a soft kiss between my brows.

Yeah, he's mine alright.

Chapter TWENTY-SIX

F amily.
  Family.
  Family.

The word echoes in my head, rapidly repeating the curse of a title. This woman, she murdered our family.

My family.

Rory, Roxy and I let out feral screams. With red in our vision, we charge but the Hound brothers stop us.

"She wants you to attack mindlessly. That's not your family!" Draven yells at us as we fight their holds.

"I feel the kinship, Dray! Move or I will fight you!" Rory hisses in his face but our men won't budge.

"That may well be family but they will attack you and we don't know what they're capable of. What if you kill one of them by accident or you get killed?" Drug shakes me as he says the words.

I know he's right but I can't *not* do anything. I want that bitch's head on a spear!

The monsters begin charging us, but in unison. Drug and his brothers shoot their flames, creating a barrier between us and them. The monsters don't stop though, they leap high over the flames forcing the brothers to let us go and fight them off.

"To Merelda, sisters!"

We shift into Crows and fly high above the reaching hands of the monsters as Drug, Drac and Draven keep them distracted. We swoop low while dodging the orbs and stakes Merelda throws at us. Each time one of us is closer, we rip and tear at her scalp and hair but we can't find an opening to actually land and do some real damage.

I sweep low to the ground, coming up to her back when she turns and hits me with something like a block of ice right on my left wing. I shift into my cobra and slither with unnatural speed below another orb, ready to strike her legs but as I ready for the bite, something grabs my tail.

The delicate bones in a real snake would snap and break under the pressure the monster is using but my cobra's bones are almost like carbon fiber, practically unbreakable. I spin and strike the creature on instinct but let go before I actually kill the thing. Instead of fighting the beast, I wrap him or her, it's difficult to tell what the gender of the creatures are, and squeeze around its neck and arms. I use my muscles to cut off the blood flow to its brain until it passes out then I shift back to my natural form.

Everyone is fighting, the men hold off any more monsters coming at us while trying not to kill them, though I do see some laying still on the ground and my heart breaks. My sisters and Darren continue to fight Merelda, looking for an advantage while opening wounds on her but they heal almost as soon as they appear.

In a rage, I grab the horn of the unconscious monster at my feet and break it off near the skull. I hope that didn't hurt the person under the fucked up curse.

I turn back to Merelda and throw the horn as hard as I can at her back. The pointed bone sails through the air and I watch as it hits its mark on her lower back, leaving a gaping hole big enough for a fist to fit through.

I charge at her as she falls to her knees but Elsie's voice, unnaturally loud, screams at everyone to stop.

"Grandmother! I'm here and I have your betrayer!"

Everyone stops, including the monsters, who back up to Merelda.

Elsie stands at the door with a bleeding Mayfly at her feet. He looks like he's dead with blood and lacerations all over his face and back. Elsie has the most vicious look on her face and when her brothers move to her she blasts them back with an invisible force from her hand.

What the hell is happening? Did the potion wear off?

I run right for her and jump when she throws her hand in my direction. I feel the blast of energy flow beneath my body and Elsie's eyes widen as I land before her. She's no longer a little girl so I swing, aiming to knock her unconscious but her self-preservation kicks in.

She lets Mayfly's collar go and blocks my attack while giving me a few of her own. Some of our punches land as others miss their mark but we don't trade hits for long, in my haste to stop her, she uses her magic to drag Mayfly to Merelda.

"Noo! Elsie, fight her influence! Don't do this to your mate!" I scream as I land a blow to her stomach. She weaves her fingers as she doubles over and suddenly I'm wrapped tightly with invisible ropes.

Merelda cackles loudly as she leans over to deliver a killing blow to Mayfly with a curved dagger. Just before the blade reaches him, Mayfly rolls to his back, Nymph features on display.

He pushes off the ground while gripping her upper arm and her hand which clutches the dagger. With the loudest and most gruesome snap ever, Mayfly rips off Merelda's arm from the elbow like it's a chicken bone. While she screams in pain, he slams the dagger into her chest and then head butts her so hard it sounds like a pumpkin being smashed on the ground.

Elsie lets me go and runs for Mayfly as Merelda falls to the ground with her legs bent at odd angles. Mayfly gives Elsie a golden looking stone covered in blood and quickly she begins chanting in a language the Witches use.

I forget the monsters around us until they begin to groan and howl which makes me jump a foot in the air. I need a fucking vacation.

"Are you okay, Black?" Drug pulls me to his chest and growls at the monsters who seem to be in pain. I don't reply or do anything other than grip Drug's torn and bloodied shirt, my body is weak and the spot where ice hit me is taking a long time to heal. I just want to sit, drink some good whiskey and never move again.

The monsters start to really howl and some drop to the ground writhing in pain.

"What's happening!" I scream at Elsie.

"She's releasing the curse on these people!" Mayfly shouts back as he guards Elsie's back. Who knows what these creatures will do to stop the pain despite the fact that she's trying to help them.

"Oh my fangs! Look!" Roxy shouts jumping up and down in Drac's arms as he tries to use his body to protect the little China doll.

I snicker in my mind at the sight but I quickly suck in a sharp breath when I look at what she's pointing to. The monster near her and every one of the monsters closest to Elsie, begin to vibrate so fast while flakes and dust fall from them. Just like the movie Silent Hill, the grotesque exterior of the beasts fall away and out of the ashes rises Blood Crow from ages gone by.

Generations of Crows stand and look at their hands and bodies. Some touch their faces while others sob in relief. I don't want to look around, I don't want to hope but I can't stop myself from searching the small crowd for the two faces I remember from my childhood memories. Two people I thought didn't love me or my sisters enough to stick around.

"Ronny?"

My heart beats out of my chest at the familiar voice coming from behind me. I'm shaking as I grip Drug tighter to me, afraid to turn, afraid to see the one whom I've needed all these centuries.

"Skunk?"

I spin at the name I haven't heard since I was a babe and standing before me, looking haggard and wasted, is my father.

I fall to my knees and cover my mouth but nothing can hold back the broken sob that wracks my body, shaking my ribs with so much force it becomes painful.

"Papa?" My voice is barely a whisper but my father hears it nonetheless. He staggers in place like my childhood endearment has hit him just as strong as my nickname hit me. Drug rushes over to him and catches him, bringing him to me.

I should stand and hold my father. I should scream with delight and wrap my arms around him but I don't. I've been in need of my father's arms for so long, in need of a hug *from* him. I think he knows because he drops to his knees and wraps me in the most tender hug I've ever received.

My sisters tackle us to the ground and hold us with sobs filling the air.

"I never thought I'd see you girls again."

My father's voice is hoarse but to me, there's no sweeter sound.

Chapter
TWENTY-SEVEN
DRUG HOUND

E lsie drops to her hands and knees as Mayfly holds her hair
back.

I'm going to check on Elsie, Black.

I mentally tell Ronny as I leave her and her sisters to the
reunion they deserve. I know what it's like to have your family
reunited. Having my sister back with us is more than I could have
ever hoped for. I know my parents are gone but having Elsie brings
them back too and I'll forever be grateful for that.

Drac and Draven run beside me and we stop near our sister who
is retching in the grass. The stone Mayfly used is glowing brightly
with multiple colors and Merelda violently shakes beside it.

Not giving a shit about the fluids on the ground, I drop next to
Elsie as our brothers hover over Merelda, ready to strike if she
comes to.

"That was a stupid and brave thing you did, sister," I grind out.
I know she did it to save the Crow ancestors but Merelda is an

unspeakable monster and losing Elsie would have killed us. And since we can't actually die, it would have been a tortuous existence.

She wipes at her mouth and chuckles at me, "You need to remember, Drug. I'm not the baby you once knew. If I can stop someone from hurting those I love I will always dive in, no matter the threat to myself."

I mime wringing her neck but smile all the same. She's definitely a Hound, stubborn and bullheaded.

I look over to Mayfly and see nothing but admiration in his gaze as he brushes hair back from my sister's face. He will still need to prove to us that he will love and fight for my sister but I think he has proven himself today. Although, brothers like us will need daily proof no matter how long we live for.

"What happens now?" Drac asks with a lip curled in Merelda's direction. She continues to convulse but there's no sign she'll stop.

She can be killed now but in order for her to stay dead, we'll need to wait for the full moon. Until then, she will need to be encased in glass. It'll keep her energy enclosed until then. Her power is in the stone, it will leave the stone and find someone new to inhabit when her spirit is no longer living."

"Drug?" Ronny's voice stops me from commenting that Merelda is no Disney character and she should be kept in a coffin or something.

I turn to her voice and smile at her. She looks incredibly shy and it makes me want to tease her but I know this is overwhelming for her. Shit, it's overwhelming for me.

"Drug, this is my dad, Amos Crow. Dad, this is my mate, Drug... Hound."

Her father doesn't blink an eye at hearing my last name, the name of their mortal enemies, he just grabs my hand and pulls me in for a hug. He's a lot stronger than he appears. I can feel all his bones beneath his skin and I cringe at how hard I've hugged him. That would be just great if I broke this man's back after just meeting him.

We pull apart and he clears his throat. His voice is terribly cracked and broken as he speaks but I can hear the sincerity in each word he speaks.

"Thank you for fighting for my daughters. I didn't want to attack them and I will forever be in your debt for protecting them."

"Well, sir, I'm not built to lie so I'll be honest. I was mostly protecting Black Bird. Your other daughters are whack jobs, sir," I say this with a chuckle amid punches from the sisters but their father just laughs at it.

"Thank you nonetheless." He claps my shoulder as Rory and Roxy introduce him to my brothers.

Ronny jumps in my arms and buries her face in my neck. I hold her close and despite all the horrors we've faced, I laugh and nip her earlobe. This is my place. I belong here with my Black Bird. I want to spend the rest of our lives in each other's arms, making each moment count to make up for all the moments that didn't.

I put Ronny back on her feet as Elsie stands and holds a hand out to Amos. It's tense for a moment but Amos has no anger for my sister. He ignores her hand and wraps his arms around her.

"Thank you for freeing us. Thank you for sacrificing your mate, I know it was a ploy but the risk was there nonetheless. You have me in your debt, True Witch."

"No, Amos. You owe me nothing. If you want to repay me, do it by making up for lost time with your daughters. The pain they've carried is as heavy as your own. I wish I could bring back every person Merelda killed."

Darren comes out with a large crate filled with packs of blood, passing them out to the fifty or so Blood Crows still coming out of their metamorphosis-like state. Each Vampire takes the packs with graciousness that you wouldn't expect. You see, I grew up in a time where witches, Vampires and Werewolves were hunted and called evil but after meeting Ronny and her sisters, I see how wrong that was.

In any race and family, no matter the realm, there are always those who break the rules of the moral compass. But looking at the ragtag of people around me, enemies coming together, it's clear that not everyone wears a crown of sin.

"Are all these people part of your family?" I ask Ronny as I watch people reunite with loved ones.

"I don't know any of them. My father says that my mother really did die while fighting Merelda when she took him so we won't be seeing Mother in this life." Ronny wipes at her eyes as she tells me this. I know she's holding her emotions in.

I top her chin up to look at me, "It's okay to break, Black Bird. I'll find ways to put you back together in the end."

She squeezes her eyes closed, pushing tears free from the confines of her lashes as she drops her face to my chest. Her body shakes as I rub her back, soothing her while she lets the emotions out. Sometimes, breaking for a moment makes you stronger. It releases something deep inside your soul and makes room for those that deserve a spot in there. We just need someone to keep us grounded while it happens.

"It's okay, Black. I got your pieces."

T he full moon will be upon us tonight and soon we will stand beneath its brilliant glow. Merelda has been held in a painful slumber filled with torture on her powerless body. This evening will bring an end to her reign of terror and bloodshed.

I've spent time with our father and bringing him up to speed on life as it is now. He's a big fan of pepperoni pizza and definitely loves the smartphones.

It was hilarious to see him hiss and snarl when I first showed him the screen with moving pictures. He kept looking behind it as if there was someone there. Showing him new things has been a delight.

Right now, we're standing cloaked as we watch cars pass by on the road. He's been standing on the street watching them pass through him with nothing but wonderment on his face.

Come on, Pops! I want to show you the ice cream parlor. The owner is Fae and she always has the best frozen blood," Roxy says while clapping her hands. We each share dad throughout the day and now it's Roxy's turn. I've mostly brought my dad here because he just loves the cars that drive by. He even tries to race them like he's a little kid. Seeing him smile and find fascination in everything I've taken for granted is the best thing I've ever witnessed.

He kisses me on the cheek before leaving, "See you tonight, Skunk."

"See ya, Pop."

Once he leaves, I focus on Drug and his energy before siphoning myself to him. He's been out with his brothers showing Elsie around but we spend the evenings together every day. It's been a good few weeks getting to know him and learning who he is when we're not searching for talisman and fighting evil witches with chips on their shoulders.

I've learned that he's an incredible chess player who can beat any one of us in under five moves. I learned that his favorite thing to eat is any kind of red meat, big shock I know. He also has to sleep on his right side or he won't be able to fall asleep. His favorite time of day is right before the sun wakes up and just as it dips below the horizon.

The past few weeks have been wonderful and some of the best memories were made recently.

I arrive in the alleyway where we first met. Drug is leaning up against the brick wall of a building as he smokes a cigarette. Yes that's right, Drug likes cancer sticks. Although, I doubt they'll be able to hurt him in any way since he's a fire breathing Hellhound and all.

"Hey girl, you come here often?"

Gah! Did I mention he has a thing for corny fucking jokes? Well, he does and they're stupid every time. Also, he's been watching movies from the nineties and I think he's definitely found his whole personality there. Works for me since he's so devilish with that body and rod of his.

Just kidding... sort of. I really do love this man. His rod and bod are just a bonus.

"Yes, I do actually. You see, this is where I'm always finding Roxy. The humans have some very ominous stories about her since the eighteen hundreds. She's been dubbed *The River Crow*," I say it low and creepy like I'm telling a scary story to a bunch of camp kids.

Drug chuckles and wraps an arms around my waste, "I don't really care about your pink haired sister. She cut me with that fucking spiked ball and chain of hers and said '*oops*.'"

I laugh at that. Roxy is a total savage and the stories about her are definitely warranted. The humans have been afraid of the large Crow that targets men who slink through the dark, harboring bad intentions for the clueless women they follow.

"Okay, so what are we doing here then, Drug?"

It's the afternoon and people will soon wander what two people are doing in the alley. As if reading my thoughts, which he didn't because I now have a block on him when I don't want him reading my head, Drug smiles and pushes me up against the wall.

"Cloak us, Black Bird."

I do and he runs his nose up the column of my throat before dipping his tongue into the two puncture marks on my neck. They haven't gone away but it's like they're connected to my labia and every time he touches them, my body comes alive with sexual desire.

"I want you, here where we first met." I moan when he grinds his hard cock against my stomach, our jeans blocking the heat of his delicious skin.

"When you first shifted here, I was instantly hard for you. You are the most sinful and beautiful creature I have ever seen."

He stops and pulls one of my breasts free from my tank top and swirls his wet tongue around my hard nipple.

"So you're saying you've seen someone better, pup?"

I can't help teasing him. He puts his fingers against my mouth and growls in my ear.

"You need to keep that mouth shut before you get it filled with my cock. Got it?"

Oh boy, his threats are treats. I open my mouth and let my shifted snake tongue slip around his fingers before sucking them in. I give him a wink as I sucking on his digits with my panther's purr rumbling in my throat.

Fuck, I'm so turned on right now.

Drug groans and pops the button on my shorts before sliding his hand in and through my wet folds. I gyrate my hips, getting that perfect friction against my throbbing clit as he slides in two fingers and pumping as hard as he can within the confines of my shorts.

I pull my shorts down a little before slipping my hand down his pants and massaging his heavy balls. I let my fingers rub against his perineum, the very sensitive space between his ass and balls while sucking his fingers harder.

"Oh fuck, Black. I want your lips wrapped around my cock. I want to fuck your throat and feel your gags on my aching dick."

Fucking crude and so sexy.

I pull my hand free and spin our positions. I kiss him hard against the wall before sliding down his body, licking his hard abs as I go.

"Then let me."

I pull his jeans down, freeing his leaking cock and grasp him tightly. I pull his balls free and suck them into my mouth, squeezing gently as I pump him the way he likes it. I keep my eyes on him as he watches me lick from base to tip, dipping my tongue into the slit at the top. His face is serene with hooded eyes while biting his lip.

He's perfect, so fucking beautiful and rugged.

I open my mouth and take him in deeply, past my uvula and down my throat as I purr. I shake my head slightly when I can't take him deeper and he lets out a sting of incoherent words as he tangles his fingers in my hair.

With my free hand I rub his balls and let him guide my head. I rub that sensitive patch of skin behind his balls and he begins to roughly fuck my throat. I love every second of it.

Just when I think he's going to come he pulls me up and pushes my chest against the wall.

"If I didn't stop you, I'd come in that fuckable mouth and I don't want to do that... yet."

Drug pulls my shorts down over my ass and slaps my cheeks. He rubs the sting out as he lines the tip of his dick up with my ass. We've done this once before and I have to say, I'm glad I've never let anyone touch me there because Drug does it so fucking good.

Slowly, Drug pushes in all the way to the hilt before he starts to fuck me hard. His big dick slides in and out, rough and fast over and over again and I'm screaming. I don't even have to touch my clit, everything his cock hits inside me is like a slap on my pussy and before I know it, my orgasm is rushing to the surface.

"That's it baby, come for your devil."

And I do. I come so hard as Drug pounds my ass like he's trying to win a medal.

His pumps become as erratic as our breaths when he finally roars and slams deep inside, shooting ropes of come.

We stand there for a few moments, catching our breaths as the sun begins to set. The colors change and create a magnificent sight along the river.

"I love you, Black."

"I love you, Drug."

We get back to the Crow house, so we can get ready to close Merelda's chapter once and for all.

At first, I thought we'd be on top of each other in this home especially with Elsie and Mr. Crow living here but the plantation house is very large. The cellar is bigger than the house as well and it's been the main living quarters for Ronny and I when she gave up her room to her father.

Overall, things have been going great and it's got me more anxious than ever.

"Where are Darren and pops?" Ronny asks Draven as we saunter through the house.

"Your dad is upstairs on the piano and Darren is with his woman. She still needs rest so he's opted to skip out on tonight's main event." Draven continues to watch the underground fighting on the tablet in his hands. Ever since Ronny showed him the mafia ring in New York he's been streaming it. He says he'll fight in it one day. Doubtful though since he has a shitty temper and will most likely kill everyone there.

"Is Audrey not doing good?" Ronny asks before entering the kitchen.

"She's fine but coming back from the dead after being decapitated is most likely taxing on the soul."

That's right ladies and gents, my sister, the motherfucking True Witch brought back Darren's mate from the dead. Elsie down plays that shit like it's nothing but come on now, that badass. Darren thinks so too. He has sworn oath to her and promised to always fight for her with the backing of the Fairies.

We enter the kitchen and find Drac, Rory and Roxy hanging out waiting for Elsie to be done with the dagger. I'm not sure what needs to be done with it but it'll assure Merelda dies indefinitely.

"Do you ever get the feeling that we're living in the calm before the storm?" Rory asks no one in particular.

"It does but maybe it's just because we've grown used to looking over our shoulders?" Ronny says hopefully.

"Possibly."

None of us seem convinced despite that being very true.

The past few weeks have been a reprieve from the problems we faced and the fears we had of losing someone to Merelda's wickedness. Battling her dark forces were no simple task but coming to the end of it all was like being reborn.

Tonight, we'll finally be able to breathe again. We'll be able to live a life we deserve with the people we love.

Speaking of love, "How are things going with your dad?" I ask the sisters.

"Good! He's learning everything with ease and excitement, it's really fun to watch him." Rory laughs.

"Yeah, you guys should have seen him at the ice cream parlor. He ordered almost every kind and ate them all. But the best part was when he got his first brain freeze. I had to cloak us when he began howling like a fucking rabid animal. God, I couldn't stop laughing." The fact that Roxy finds delight in this is absolutely disturbing but I have to admit, picturing his face is quite hilarious.

"Okay, you guys, I'm ready. Let's go kill this fuck."

Roxy snorts loudly while the rest of us smother our smiles.

"What?"

Elsie has been learning how to cuss. I know, it's a shitty fucking habit to teach someone but it's unavoidable when you live in a house of bad mouthing supernaturals. I'm pretty sure Roxy uses a curse word in every sentence.

"That's not how you use it. Let's go kill this fuck*er*." I enunciate the *er* at the end and smile when Elsie's cheeks redden.

"Whatever, let's go... *fucker*." She says it mockingly to me and everyone busts up laughing.

Whatever, I'll get her back. Having her around to tease has made my brothers and I feel like those little kids we used to be before Merelda entered our lives. I don't regret becoming a Hellhound but I do wish we had human experiences with Elsie.

Ronny and her sisters join hands so we can siphon but before they can touch anyone else, their heads jerk back, faces to the ceiling and their eyes turn white.

"Fuck, they're having a vision."

"Here comes the storm."

"I wonder if they're seeing Elsie learn how to cuss correctly?" Drac is the only one to say something ridiculous and Elsie slaps him on the arm. Dray and I however, are stuck watching the sisters. I guess we're sort of used to his crazy.

Rory's face snaps to us, "Merelda has been caught, we must find the True Witch."

I glance at Elsie and see her brow furrowed. Whoever is looking for my sister will have six motherfuckers to go through first.

Roxy's face snaps down next, "The moon is risen, let's make haste."

Okay, the way she said that gave me the chills. Can this Crow sister get any creepier?

I'm clenching my fists waiting for Ronny's vision. She sees the future and I have a sick feeling growing in my stomach.

My fears are correct when she looks at us, "If you succeed at killing me, Merelda's power will be yours, True Witch."

Fucking hell. Why does there need to be more thrown at us? Elsie walk forward and gently breaks the links the sisters have, pulling their hands away from one another.

They come to and immediately look at Elsie.

"The coven leader will be here soon. They want a duel of sorts to reclaim their rightful place at the Elder's table." Rory says stoically before looking to Draven and sharply nodding. The look of murder shines brightly in her irises.

"You can beat her, Elsie and you have the backup of the Blood Crows. Whether you want it or not, we are in your debt for freeing those whom Merelda cursed." Ronny cracks her neck and holds out her hand to Elsie the way a big sister would.

"I wonder what the Witch's blood tastes like? Maybe like spiked root beer?" I pinch the bridge of my nose at Roxy's nonsense but Drac taps his chin thoughtfully.

Whatever the case may be, we'll be ready for it.

"I'll help you find out, Rox. I'm not afraid of these witches but I would like to hear them out. Just because I'm the True Witch doesn't mean I want to become the coven leader or an Elder. I just want to make sure whoever has Merelda's power is someone who will use it wisely."

"Very diplomatic for someone who doesn't want to be an Elder," Drac says sarcastically.

"You didn't let me finish. If I see that this witch is not worthy or is filled with evil intent, I will kill her."

We all stay quiet a moment, admiration flowing through us at her kick-ass-and-take-names attitude but then Roxy speaks and you know, sort of makes it weird.

"Spiked root beers on Elsie!" She skips out the door with Drac on her heels growling and making her squeal.

Everyone runs out after them looking like kids who just finished their last day of school and are ready for summer vacation.

I, however, pull out a cigarette and light it while mumbling around it, "I live in a house of crackheads."

Chapter THIRT

The moon is high and the sky is clear of clouds, showing the twinkling stars that seem to dance in delight as we stand around the soon to be dead Merelda. I on the other hand am waiting for these witches to show up and crash the party.

I'm not itching for a fight, I honestly hope they want to make sure the True Witch isn't like Merelda, after all, they did get run off by her and most likely don't want a repeat.

If these witches want a problem though... I still have some pent up anger to spew. Mayfly seems to be thinking the same thing as his fingers continue to twitch while his eyes scan the tree line.

"Okay, let's get this over with." Elsie says as she stands next to the pyre we have Merelda laying on. I gotta give the girl some props. She went from hostage to a fighter. She is brave and willing to sacrifice anything for her family. She will always have my respect.

Elsie lifts the blade and chats out the woes of death in Romanian. It's supposed to be a respectful death and even though I don't feel Merelda deserves one, we want this done correctly.

She brings the point to the Witch's heart and plunges it deeply without hesitation as the last words of the script is said.

The ground begins to shake, not violently but in a way that shows Merelda's energy is being taken back into the earth for recycling. I certainly hope no one is unfortunate enough to be born with her wicked soul.

Elsie leaves the blade in place and stands back. We all wait for her nod before all seven of us toss our Hellfire at the dry wood beneath the body. As the flames lick along the logs and catch onto the hem of Merelda's black robe, the Witches come out of the woods around us.

They stand in silence as the pyre becomes a blaze of black flames and smoke. After minutes of staring into the flames, one speaks. The leader I presume.

"We've come seeking the True Witch. We have seen the death of Merelda, the Witch of Decay," Hmm that's a new one. Not that it doesn't fit but I haven't heard the name before.

"You seek an audience or blood?" I ask with a growl to my voice.

"It depends, Oracle. Does she intend to restore what was once ours or does she wish to kill as Merelda had?"

I bristle at that but Elsie holds her hand up, stopping me from saying anything more.

"I am the True Witch but you must show me your intent before you can take back what you gave away."

All the Witches before us are now the ones bristling at those words.

"How dare you, young witchling. You know not what you speak. Merelda took with blood..."

Elsie speaks over the leader's words, "Yes, she did. But you, as the leader of your coven, ran. You gave up without a fight when you could have had the backing of your people. You chose to hide and wait for someone else to pick up the responsibility you so hurriedly dropped. So, I say again, you must show me you are worthy of the power you seek and your place amongst the new Elders. Right now, I find you sorely lacking."

I really want to yell out, *mic drop!* But I don't. It would be fitting though.

"And you are worthy?" Someone else asks.

Elsie smiles in the direction the question came from, "A worthy one wouldn't claim it. Power is for those who are willing to bear its weight. While I can hold it, I do not seek it. If your coven chooses me I will be honored, but I will not allow bad intent to have such power. I've seen what it does to people."

The lead witch steps forward with a menacing stance. "I will try you, witchling..."

Elsie's face morphs from sweet to hellish in a heartbeat. "And you will die, old Witch."

I pull my short swords from my thigh holsters and take a stance, ready for someone to jump in unfairly but every single witch steps back along the tree line as Elsie waits for the Witch to make her move.

Like lightning, the coven leader lashes out with a glowing whip that is almost transparent but it's cut across Elsie's face shows it is definitely a solid object.

My sisters and I hiss while the brothers hold Mayfly back.

Elsie catches the whip on the Witch's next snap and uses her powers to light the weapon on fire but the leader is not deterred.

She swings her arm out and begins launching stakes at Elsie but none hit their mark. It seems that Elsie is playing with the old bat.

"Enough of your child's play!" Elsie swings her hand out and clenches her fist at the Witch before she suddenly stops moving. Must be those invisible ropes Merelda used on me.

"Yield, Witch or you will die," Elsie tells her as the other witches around us watch with their brows stuck to their hairline, but none of them seem to want a fight with the True Witch.

"I will never yield to such a..." Her words are cut off with a loud snap of her neck.

There are no gasps or outbursts of any kind from the silent witches around us. Even as Elsie uses her power to drop the body on top of Merelda, none of them speak a word.

Instead, they all turn and disappear back into the woods.

Suddenly my vision changes. No longer is my family standing before me. I'm in the same field where we burned Merelda but the sight in front of me is a bloody battle and there is a large wooden stake in the center. All around me Blood Crows and witches are killing each other and my stomach lurches at the gory sight.

"NOOOO!" I hear Drac's howl and I turn back to the center where the wooden stake is. Tied to the pole with fire licking around her is my baby sister, Roxy.

"May the River Crow die the death of a Witch!"

A scream rips through me as my vision comes back to the present. Everyone surrounds me and lifts me from my knees. But I hug Roxy close to me and make eye contact with Drac.

He must see the fear in my eyes because he rips his shirt from his chest and howls in a rage, tearing at his hair like a wild man.

Our war is not over. Making a legacy for my sisters will never be over. Well fuck that, if these Witches want a fight, they'll have to kill us all before they can lay a finger on my sister.

I'm Ronny *motherfucking* Crow and if blood is what they want, I'll pour them a river.

More Books By
V. DOMIN

SING TO ME

FIGHT FOR ME

KILL FOR ME

OMERTA: A VERY MAFIOSO CHRISTMAS

FATE'S DICE

Acknowledgments
THANK YO

There's a lot of people I'd love to thank and give a special moment to but I'll keep this short and sweet.

First, I'd love to thank my readers. You guys have been so kind and encouraging throughout this entire process. I've received emails and DMs of everyone wanting to beta for me and help me through the writing stages. I've gotten beautiful edits by some of you and I can't even express how much joy that's given me.

There's very few people who are personally in my life and one of them is author Eleanor Aldrick. Not only is she an amazing author but she is also one of the sweetest people on this planet. She's been with me through it all and while I haven't met her in person, it's as if I've known her for years. She's known as titi Eleanor to my daughters and she'll always have a place in my heart. I highly recommend her debut series, Men Of Wrath. So good and book three will be here soon and I'm completely in love with it. Yeah, that's right, I get the first view of her talent!

Next is Jess Fondry. My lemon drop. She's been a big supporter of mine since day one and she never fails to check on me everyday. We send random texts to each other, mostly consisting of terrible memes and crazy TikTok videos. I'm her girlboy lamoooo! If you don't know who she is, I recommend you go check out her series, The Beacon Hills. It's available on Amazon and Kindle Unlimited!

My betas! You guys are a powerful group. You ladies helped me to make sure this book is what you read today and I'm eternally grateful. Roxy Medina, you're a bombass queen amongst queens and I'll forever praise your edits. My LSO.

Last but not least, my biggest supporter, my husband and best friend, Gabe. You're a crazy man, babe but I love you with every fiber. I'll never grow tired of you! Thank you for dealing with fast food and late nights. <3

Made in the USA
Middletown, DE
26 October 2023

41446102R00130